THE VISITOR

Vampire Erotica

mischief

Mischief
An imprint of HarperCollins*Publishers*
77–85 Fulham Palace Road,
Hammersmith, London W6 8JB

www.mischiefbooks.com

A Paperback Original 2013

First published in Great Britain in ebook format by
HarperCollins*Publishers* 2012

A catalogue record for this book is
available from the British Library

ISBN-13: 9780007553136

Find out more about HarperCollins and the environment at
www.harpercollins.co.uk/green

CONTENTS

Amuse-Bouche
Janine Ashbless

It was a dream, a nightmare, a fairy tale.

'Rose, wake up.'

She woke with no coherent memory of where she was, aware only that it was raining because she could hear it drumming on the car roof, and that her neck ached from dozing off at an awkward angle. A waft of cooler air carried a fresh dampness to her lungs, dispelling the warm fug of the vehicle interior.

'Come on.' It was the woman: that silver bobbed hair, those high and delicate cheekbones belying her age. Rose tried to marshal her memories. Amanda, wasn't it? She'd called herself Amanda and she'd been the one driving. Now she was standing at the far door and holding it open, oblivious – it seemed – to the weather.

'Where are we?' Rose looked around, confused. Through the rain-blurred night she saw white-plastered walls, illuminated windows and the base of a round turret. And a lit archway, within which a dark figure flickered momentarily. Yes, there'd been a man in the back with her, hadn't there? *What was his name? Something French*, she thought, though he'd sounded English. An edge of accusation crept into her voice: 'Is this Paris? You said you'd take me to Paris.'

'We're a few kilometres outside Paris.' Water dripped from Amanda's pale hair. 'This is a hotel.'

'Why've we stopped?' Kyle would be wondering what was keeping her – she couldn't keep him waiting, could she?

'For dinner. Aren't you hungry?'

Oh, of course – Kyle wasn't expecting her. She hadn't told him she was coming because she wanted it to be a wonderful surprise. She hadn't told anyone about her plan to hitch-hike across the English Channel and then all the way to Kyle's student digs in Paris. But yes, she was hungry. She'd been living on crisps for the last twenty-four hours. Crisps and that horrible ham sandwich on the ferry, while she was hiding in the ladies' toilet waiting for that lorry driver with the creeping hands to give up on waiting for her.

Still dizzy with sleep, Rose emerged into the rain. Cold drops licked her lips. She'd been dreaming, she remembered. Something about kissing Kyle ... only, his lips had been icy.

'I can't,' she said, hunching against the downpour as Amanda came round the back of the car. The white walls of the chateau loomed like a fairy-tale castle and steam rose from the exterior up-lights in miniature mist wreathes. 'I mean, I haven't got that sort of money.'

'Don't worry about that. We've got it covered.' Amanda took her arm. 'Come on.'

The night was horrible and Rose obeyed, letting herself be led towards the arched doorway.

Inside, it was a palace: panelled walls, gilt furniture carved with grapes and cherubs, huge vases of flowers, enormous portraits of ugly people in beautiful clothes. The carpet under Rose's feet was so thick she felt like she was sinking into it. Her jaw dropped. She'd only ever seen this sort of opulence on a school trip to Windsor Castle. She'd never imagined that real people stayed in places like this, and somehow it made her feel less real herself.

The man was there, talking in French to a stout, elegant woman who wore an expression of stiff hauteur. He glanced at them as they drew near, and smiled. For a moment Rose couldn't help thinking the smile was for her, and her heart bumped. He was really not bad-looking for an older bloke – he must be in his thirties, she guessed – and his smile lit his dark eyes. Then she realised that the pleasure must be intended for Amanda, of course. His girlfriend. Auntie. Whatever.

She blushed.

3

Reynauld. That was his name. She remembered now. Her mind seemed to be all over the place, like a flock of pigeons scattered by the shadow of something dark overhead.

'The room at the top of the stairs,' he murmured to Amanda, with a tilt of his head to indicate the direction. 'They'll fetch the bags.'

'This way, Rose.'

She let herself be shepherded to the foot of a great marble staircase, and it was only a chance glimpse through a pair of double doors that made her pause. The room beyond those doors was clearly a dining area. People in fine clothes sat below glittering chandeliers while waiters hovered.

'I thought we were going to eat?'

Amanda, one step higher by this point, laughed, the fine skin around her eyes creasing. 'You can't sit in those wet clothes, can you? Not in there! Come on – we've got the use of a room to freshen up in. And I can lend you one of my dresses. You must be soaked.'

It was true. Rose was sodden all down her back and her shoes squelched even on this luxurious carpet. She'd been walking through the rain in Calais port for some time before those two stopped to offer her a lift. The prospect of being able to dry herself and maybe comb her hair out was very appealing. So much so that she'd climbed two flights of steps before it dawned on her how odd it was that she and Amanda were both wet from the short walk from the car, but, as far as she could recall, Reynauld hadn't looked even slightly damp.

Maybe he'd taken the only umbrella. Not much of a gentleman, then.

Amanda showed her into a room that took her breath away. *Not a room: a suite*, she thought, spying a second chamber opening from the first through connecting doors. *They must be totally loaded.* There were flowers everywhere again, and ugly expensive furniture uphol-stered in red-and-cream stripes. The cover of the huge bed was crimson and mounded with tasselled cushions and bolsters.

'Warm yourself up with a nice hot shower,' Amanda suggested. 'I'll wait for my bag.'

There were even flowers in the bathroom: white lilies that gave off a sweet narcotic scent. Huge fluffy towels too, and gilt taps. Rose, alone at last, shook her head and giggled, bemused by everything from the bidet to the matched range of expensive-looking toiletries on the marble sink. Guests didn't even have to bring their own hairbrushes – there were two laid out already. There wasn't a lock on the inside of the bathroom door though. *Ugh, how French*, she thought. But the chance to indulge was too tempting to resist.

Oh, it was so good to shed her damp and frowsty clothes and step into a piping-hot shower. She was especially delighted to discover the many nozzles that sprayed her with water from multiple angles and she spent time playing with them until she got them to hit her just right – on the upper slopes of her breasts and right over her pubic mound. The naughtiness made her giggle, and the teasing insistent pressure made her wish Kyle were there, soaping her up with that expensive body-crème and running his fingers through the suds.

Soon, she promised herself, sighing and shivering with pleasure. *I'm nearly there.*

It was a bit of a shock to find, when she stepped out, that all her clothes had vanished off the bathroom floor. In their stead, a pale violet-grey slip and a pair of stockings had been draped over the dressing-table chair. Rose frowned. She hadn't noticed anyone entering the bathroom; she hadn't heard a thing. It was like a fairy tale, where things appeared by magic.

She wondered whether to march out in her towel and demand her clothes back, but decided to try the new ones on first.

The result was disconcerting. She stood before the mirror and stared at herself, in that slip that barely skimmed her thighs and the hold-ups in their matching hue. Her skin was cream-pale and the tiny gold cross Kyle had given her gleamed upon her breastbone. The lingerie made her look older; not in a bad way, but more sophisticated. *Like a model*, she thought. The silk clung to her breasts and hips to emphasise her slender figure. She wondered if she ought to have a matching pair of panties with those same embroidered white flowers on, or whether it was just gross to wear someone else's knickers. *Am I supposed to go down to dinner with a bare pussy then?*

She was combing out her wet hair when Amanda walked in.

'There,' she said, coming up behind Rose in the mirror. 'That colour suits you better than it does me. I just look so washed out these days.' Without asking permission, she adjusted the straps at Rose's shoulders and smoothed the slip over her waist and hips. Rose was both flattered and irritated. She thought she looked better than Amanda too. *Of course I do – I'm much younger for a start.* And why was the woman resting her hands on her shoulders, like she owned Rose? After that hot shower, Amanda's fingers felt chilly.

'You and Reynauld,' she said, pouting her lips and looking with satisfaction at her reflection. 'Is he your boyfriend then?'

'My employer. And yes. We are lovers.'

Ugh. She's got to be at least forty. What does he see in her? And what a snotty way she has of talking, like she thinks she's the Queen or something. 'Aren't you, like, a bit old for him?'

Amanda didn't answer for a moment and Rose, looking

at her narrowed eyes, had time to wonder if maybe she'd been a bit rude, before the other woman said softly, 'He's older than he looks.'

'Is he French?' Rose decided not to dwell on her possible faux pas. 'He looks French.'

'He's from Baghdad originally, I believe.'

'What, he's an Arab sheikh?' Rose was tickled and a bit alarmed by the prospect of such exoticism and wealth.

'Persian, not Arab. And not a sheikh.'

'What does he do, then?'

Amanda blinked and dropped her gaze. 'He used to work in the City. We're … currently relocating.'

Banker, said Rose to herself: *Boring*. 'Are we going to eat, then?'

'Yes. We're going to eat. Come on through.'

Amanda held the door and Rose preceded her into the bedroom. Half a dozen steps in, the girl realised that Reynauld was there, sitting on the bed with his hands at his sides, waiting for them. Rose stopped dead, shock rippling across her skin. Against the crimson bedspread he looked as dark as a clot of congealed blood. His black shirt was open so she could see his bare chest, and there was a look of patient anticipation on his face.

As Amanda's hands descended on her shoulders once more, cold and implacable, Rose felt all the air leave her lungs and her brain solidify into a solid useless mass. She couldn't stop looking at Reynauld's torso. He had black hair etched across his chest and his flat hard stomach – not at all like Kyle, whose lithe body was smooth like polished wood, or like a girl's. There was nothing remotely feminine about this man, and Rose found herself appalled.

'Come here,' he said. His voice was soft and deep, like the voice of darkness itself. But not cool like Amanda's: warm with pleasure instead. His black eyes drank her in, as if he were sucking the light from her. Rose felt the hands at her shoulders push her forward. Her heart was rocketing with dread and with realisation: that this was what it had all been about, that this was what they had been planning since they stopped to give her a lift in Calais. And though she felt sick with fear and raw with betrayal, at exactly the same time there was a flush of wet and terrible heat between her legs, as if this was what she had been waiting for too.

'What do you think?' asked Amanda.

'Very nice,' he answered, and then dashed any thought that his approval might have been aimed at Rose herself by adding, 'Show me her breasts.'

Deftly Amanda swept the thin straps off Rose's shoulders and reached round to heft her breasts from the fallen silk. Rose's nipples swelled to hard puckers of protest under the brush of her chill fingertips, and her thighs squirmed, trying to staunch the moisture welling there.

'Please,' she said breathlessly, lifting her hands.

Amanda batted them away and cupped her breasts, pressing into her from behind with her own body. She was surprisingly strong. Rose found herself pushed forward almost into Reynauld's reach.

'Small tits,' said Amanda apologetically.

'Beautiful,' answered Reynauld. Lust was like a thick black tide brimming in his eyes and his voice. Rose could feel it sucking at her, and she knew that if he touched her she'd be pulled under and drowned. 'Rose,' he murmured, 'thank you for this.'

In addressing her, it was as if he gave her permission to emerge from her blank white shock and find words. 'You can't do this,' she said, her voice shaky. Then: 'I've got a boyfriend, you know.'

It was the stupidest of excuses and she saw amusement crease the corners of his eyes. 'Don't worry,' he promised. 'It'll be our little secret.' He didn't bother to hide the mockery as his lip curled and revealed an eyetooth like a knife-point.

'Oh, Christ,' she moaned.

Reynauld lifted a brow as if in mild disapproval of her blasphemy. 'Take the necklace off.'

At once Amanda released her breasts and delved under her hair at the nape of her neck.

'That's Kyle's!' said Rose, as the catch resisted at first, then broke in the woman's hands. The chain slid down between her breasts and struck the carpet.

'Tell me about Kyle,' he said, his gaze enveloping hers. 'Tell me what you like to do with him.'

She couldn't. As she looked into the black depths of his gaze the warm darkness in him flowed into her, and she couldn't remember Kyle. Not his face or his voice or anything she thought about him. There was only this man, Reynauld.

'Do you enjoy making love together?'

'Yes.' She knew it was true, though she could recall no loving emotion. Just the lust. There was nothing else when she looked into Reynauld's eyes except lust – and surrender. She could feel the hot gather of her juices overflowing their cup and slicking her labia.

'Which position, Rose?'

'All of them.'

'Do you like to suck his cock?'

'Yes.'

'What about when he eats you?'

'Yes,' she answered, though she knew she was only gifting him the cruellest of punchlines.

He beckoned her with a crooked finger, and as she stepped unresisting between his knees he laid his hands upon her waist, caressing the smooth lines there. His fingers were cold too, but there was a perfect certainty in them. 'Do you like it,' he murmured, his lips parted hungrily, 'when Kyle sucks your breasts?'

'Yes,' she said, trembling in his grasp. She felt Amanda's

hands close around her wrists and draw them back – the grip was not cruel, but it was unbreakable and she knew what it meant. And with her final admission, as if she no longer had any excuse or defence, his mouth closed upon her right nipple.

Teeth punctured skin. The pain was as sharp and exquisite as orgasm and Rose arched, gasping aloud. She felt his hands slide up round her back. Then the searing pain became a pleasure just as keen, just as jagged, racing through her capillaries and flooding her senses. Her breast felt as if it were swelling beneath his ravenous kiss, red-hot against his cold tongue. He bit her over and over, lightly and almost tenderly, and then he shifted to her other breast and bestowed the same benison, tugging and sucking the swollen point.

Rose sobbed with every tug and every pulse, panting wildly. She looked down at herself. She saw his dark head and his black lashes. She saw his clothes fall away from his shoulders, disintegrating to wisps and then to nothing, as if they were only woven of smoke, so that without the least effort he was suddenly naked. She glimpsed the bright smear of crimson, and then she shut her eyes and took refuge from that sight in the sensations that coursed through her, overwhelming all other instincts – even fear.

'Now,' said Reynauld thickly. He shifted and turned her to face outwards, pulling her down into his lap and spreading her legs. She felt his hard chest against her back, the rasp of his legs against her silk-clad thighs, and then the nudge of his erection between them in that soft wet open cleft. With one arm he held her; with the other hand he guided his cock to its target. She thought she was so slick she should have been able to take him easily, but his girth came as a shock and she gasped as it stretched her.

'My Amanda does not yet have her new teeth,' he said, his voice wet, working his way into Rose with consummate, implacable care, his fingers dancing on her clit now. 'So I must bite for her. But you will find her kisses just as sweet as mine.'

Drunk with arousal, Rose could hardly focus on what she saw before her: Amanda in her austere grey dress, her delicate face a mask of hunger; Amanda kneeling before the two of them and nuzzling up to her breasts, sucking and lapping at the runnels of blood. But Rose surely felt it – the same thrill that raced from the puncture wounds like liquid lightning, all the way to her clit and her burning core. Her arousal gathered like a thunderhead as he impaled her to the hilt.

Then Reynauld caught her head and drew it back against his shoulder. She hung between orgasm and terror. She'd seen the movies; she knew he was going to bite out her exposed throat. His cold breath swept her neck and cheek and ear.

'Give it up to me, Rose. Give it all up. Let my beloved taste your pleasure as you surrender to me – ah, yes.'

Disobedience was never a possibility. Rose broke like a storm, and tears ran down her face as she howled.

But he didn't bite. To her indescribable relief and disappointment, he did not touch her throat. Instead, as Amanda lifted her face to show a scarlet lip-stain that looked garish against her porcelain pallor, he took Rose's whole limp weight in his hands and began to slide her up and down on the cock impaling her.

'Wait,' said Amanda. 'I know what you want.' Taking Rose's hands, she drew the girl to her feet, right off Reynauld, and turned her to face him again. A push on Rose's shoulders dropped her to her knees. 'Suck his cock,' Amanda ordered.

Reynauld's expression filled with consternation, almost dismay – which Rose might have found baffling if her attention had not been fixed on other parts. His stiffly erect cock made Kyle's look like a toy. She would hardly have believed that it had all been inside her, if it hadn't been for the glistening evidence painted the length of its shaft.

'Amanda, this isn't –' he said, his teeth bared like an attack-dog's.

'You want it,' Amanda answered. She caught Rose's hair and pushed her head to his cock. 'Take it in your mouth.'

Overbalancing, Rose grabbed his thighs. Hair ran rough beneath her palms. *Oh fuck, he's so ...* she cried inside her head. There was hair on his legs, his chest and his belly, as black and glistening as lines drawn in fresh ink. He was all muscle beneath it too, his thighs hard like stone and just as cold. She'd never touched a body like it. It made her feel ignorant and tiny. She opened her lips to the bell of his cock as Amanda forced her head down upon it, and tasted her own pussy on him.

Reynauld made no more protestations.

'Take it all in,' Amanda commanded.

Oh, God, there was no way on earth she could get that thing in all the way to the root. She laved him with her tongue, trying to make it more slippery and manageable, but Amanda pushed her right down until he butted the back of her throat. For a long moment she couldn't draw breath. Then with a tug Amanda brought her back up for air, just before she started to panic.

That was all that was required of her: to make her mouth welcoming. Amanda controlled the speed and rhythm. Reynauld's hips jerked to urge his cock a little deeper every time. Her jaw began to ache from his girth, but she couldn't stop. Her breasts burned. She longed for him to bite them again. She hurt with the need for it.

As if he heard her wish, he reached down and pinched her nipples between his fingers and thumbs. Those buds of flesh were still as hot as if they'd been stung by wasps, and his touch was icy. It was torture, and it was what she needed. She felt herself open up, every part of her:

cunt and throat all at once. She felt his thigh muscles jump beneath his skin as his length surged right into her throat, and then he let loose a cold flood of semen.

Gasping for breath, she jerked herself free, his come running out of the corners of her mouth. Reynauld stared down at her, his bulk filling her vision. Then he snatched her right up off the floor and threw her on the bed. All teeth and cock, he wrenched her thighs apart and fell upon her pussy. Wrapping his mouth over her pubis, he bit down hard.

Rose screamed. There was no distinction between terror and pain and pleasure in that cry; they were simultaneous and overwhelming. Then they too were overborne by the great supernova of her orgasm. She kept on coming as he fed, glutting himself on her ecstasy. She clutched the coverlet and bucked her hips and kicked against him – with utter lack of effect – until Amanda crawled up on to the bed to face him.

Reynauld lifted his head then, his mouth leaking crimson. Amanda went to him, licking his lips – *like a puppy to a big dog*, thought Rose through the fog that blurred her mind. At that instant her whole picture of them flipped inside out. *He* is *old*, she thought, not with contempt but with a kind of vertigo. *He's so much older than her.* And he fed her, letting her suck from his mouth, until the two of them moved into a full kiss whose unselfconscious absorption made Rose ache with jealousy.

In her need she moaned out loud.

Reynauld remembered her then. 'Drink,' he told Amanda, drawing her down to the open pussy he had abandoned. Amanda shifted to straddle Rose's supine torso, head to tail, her knees either side of the younger woman's shoulders, her wicked three-inch heels slicing the air, her tight skirt and neat ass filling Rose's field of view. But Rose didn't care; she had what she wanted – a mouth on her clit once more, sucking.

She didn't even care when Reynauld tugged that skirt right up – revealing dove-grey stockings, slim thighs and a lack of panties equivalent to her own – even though she'd never confronted another woman's pussy before. Amanda's sex was perfectly shaven, its lips plump and glistening. In the welter of her own ecstatic turmoil, Rose forgot to be disgusted. And the sight of Reynauld's thighs eclipsing the light as he moved up behind his protégée and spread her cunt with his fingers made Rose come again.

There, inches above her face, he put his cock to Amanda's slit and speared her, ramming home with a determination nearly brutal. Amanda moaned into Rose's pussy and pushed back on to the shaft impaling her, begging for more.

'Oh!' Rose gasped, arching her neck and licking at Reynauld's swinging balls. He laughed out loud then, a sound so deep and harsh that it sounded like a snarl.

She saw it all. Every slap of his dark and hairy thighs up against Amanda's pale smooth ones. Every inch of his thick cock as it slid in and out of her split pussy, wet with her juices. Every jiggle of his ball-sac as it bounced back and forth – though soon enough it stopped swinging and tightened up to a hard knot of intent. For Rose the sight was all one with the awful, racking joy of being fed upon.

And when Reynauld came once more, his fingers biting into Amanda's ass, his thighs a shuddering tattoo that ended in slamming blows and straining stillness, she saw that too. When Reynauld pulled out, she saw his cream spilling from Amanda's sex in a slow wash. Then Amanda sat back on Rose's face and the girl saw no more, not until she'd swallowed every mouthful of Reynauld's seed and Amanda had ground out her own orgasm on Rose's face.

She thought it would be over, after that. Her body was a trembling slick of exhaustion and pleasure. But she had to wake up when Amanda tugged her back into a sitting position.

'Come on, Rose. On your feet.'

'What are we doing?' she mumbled, unable to focus her eyes.

'Going down to dinner, like we planned,' said Reynauld's deep, warm voice. 'They should have cleared the dining room of other guests by now. The food here is supposed to be excellent. Amanda still eats solids. And you will need to keep your strength up. You've a long night ahead of you.'

'What?' She blinked herself properly awake in time to see the shadows crawl out of the corners of the room and from under the furniture and creep up his limbs, arranging themselves into a reasonable facsimile of sombre clothing. Hiding his still rock-hard erection.

'Did you think we'd finished?' Amanda smiled as, ignoring all that, she tugged Rose's silk slip back up into place for her, covering up her breasts though not the jut of her engorged nipples. 'That was only an appetiser. We're still *very* hungry.'

Rose had a sudden intense vision of herself laid out on a hotel table under the horrified, avid eyes of the waiters, as Reynauld and Amanda fucked her and sucked her, turn and turn about, until she died of it. At the thought her pussy tingled, moistening anew.

It would be wonderful.

She didn't resist when Amanda took her hand and led her to the door like a child, though her legs were so shaky she had to lean on the older woman. Her breasts and pussy were heavy and aching. The touch of Reynauld's palm on her ass only made her tremble with anticipation. But just before leaving the chamber she stopped abruptly. They were facing one of the big gilt-framed mirrors. She could see herself in it, slender and waiflike and debauched in her stockings and slip, with the bloodstains leaking into the silk over her breasts. She could see Amanda clearly too: improbably neat and pristine after their tussle. But where Reynauld should be behind her there was only a shadowy distortion in the glass.

Oh, God. It's all real. Everything they say about them. 'You don't show up in the mirror,' she blurted.

She recognised the flash of Amanda's eyes: a swift, protective anger. She turned, expecting to see a similar rage in Reynauld and already flinching.

But he didn't look angry. She couldn't begin to identify his expression, only knowing that in that moment he somehow looked more human than at any point previously.

'Only light is reflected, Rose,' he told her, his voice low. 'Only light.'

* * *

Rose woke alone to breakfast in bed and a taxi waiting downstairs to take her to the Sorbonne. She had no memory of how she came to be in a beautiful Michelin-starred French hotel. Or how she'd lost three days. None whatsoever.

It was just like a fairy tale.

* * *

Author's note: Amanda and Reynauld appear in Red Grow the Roses, *by Janine Ashbless*

20

A Girl's Got to Eat
Aishling Morgan

'But I don't want to feed Aunt Isabella!' Cicely stormed.

'Don't pout,' the Baroness told her. 'It's not ladylike.'

'Somebody has to,' Florence added, 'and it is your turn, Cicely.'

'It always seems to be my turn,' Cicely answered, folding her arms across her chest. 'When do *I* get to feed, that's what I'd like to know?'

'You've been doing very well for yourself,' the Baroness said, 'at least to judge by your embonpoint.'

'We must share what bounty we are given,' Florence stated, 'for the good of all, and not only are you better equipped to provide than either of us, but your name is at the head of the rota.'

Cicely didn't trouble to answer, sparing only a brief downward glance for the way her chest bulged from the top of her corset before turning to stare out across the moonlit lawn. The cedars and the turrets and chimneys of the house created oddly shaped shadows on the grass, while a faint breeze was making the leaves of the beeches clack and their branches creak, all of which would have been very pleasant were it not for the intransigence of her companions. The Baroness was bad enough, with her superior airs and malicious humour, but Florence was worse by far, with her firm but reasonable tone and irrefutable arguments.

None of the three spoke for some time, each thinking her own thoughts and listening to the sounds of the night. The Baroness, as always, had dressed for the evening and in garments she felt correct for her age and status: a long, high-necked gown of black silk, black boots with a sharp heel, gloves and a tall hat from which depended a veil, all black save for a spray of feathers that showed a hint of dark, iridescent green. Florence, in a sense, was no less formal, in the flowing white shroud she'd been buried in a hundred and forty years previously. Cicely had dressed for town, in a corset of brilliant-green satin, voluminous split-seam drawers, stockings and smart brown shoes decorated with brass buckles.

'I should go,' she said. 'It's fully dark, and the traffic will have died down a little.'

'Not until you've fed Aunt Isabella,' the Baroness insisted. 'And, besides, you can't go out like that. You're in danger of popping out, and your hair is a bird's nest!'

'It's the fashion,' Cicely explained, 'and, besides, I need a man, or a woman, maybe, some nice, plump, baby vamp who'll let me lick –'

The Baroness drew herself up. 'Manners, Cicely! In my day –'

'In your day,' Cicely interrupted, 'I could have bought myself a prostitute for less than a shilling and done as I pleased with her, but I don't suppose you ever did that?'

'One does not remark on such things,' the Baroness answered in her most glacial tones.

'What about that nice Rococo boy?' Florence put in hastily. 'Aren't you seeing him any more?'

'Goth,' Cicely corrected. 'Marco is a Goth, and no I'm not. He was getting too weird.'

'Too weird?' the Baroness queried. 'Strange, coming from you.'

'He wanted us to sleep in a coffin,' Cicely explained, 'half full of earth.'

'I can't understand why people do that,' Florence said. 'It's desperately uncomfortable, and, besides, the whole idea of a coffin is to keep the earth out.'

'I used to have a beautiful coffin,' the Baroness mused. 'It was padded throughout the interior, even on the underside of the lid, in crimson velvet, with my coat of arms worked in gold leaf. Wretched peasants!'

'You have to see their point of view,' Cicely retorted. 'I am only too well acquainted with their point of view,' the Baroness snapped back. 'Now go and feed Aunt Isabella. I don't want to have to tell you again.'

'Yes, do, Cicely, darling,' Florence added. 'It is your turn.'

'I don't want to! You know what she's like!'

'A little eccentric, I grant you, but you normally rather like that sort of thing.'

'Not before she's fed! Look, I'll do it when I get back.'

'Now,' the Baroness insisted. 'You are beginning to try my patience, Cicely St Cyr.'

'Don't start that again, please,' Cicely answered. 'I am more than one hundred and ten years old, and –'

'Do as you are told,' the Baroness said firmly, 'or you will have to be spanked.'

'Isn't it really about time you stopped doing that sort of thing?' Cicely demanded. 'This is the twenty-first century.'

'So it is, my dear,' the Baroness answered, 'but you and I belong to the nineteenth, and I see no reason to change our behaviour.'

'I do!' Cicely exclaimed, but it was already too late. A pale, bony hand had shot out, to grab hold of her arm. She was quickly drawn in, her squalling protests ignored as she was hauled into place across the Baroness' knee, her skirts turned up, her drawers pulled open and her rounded, milk-white bottom soundly spanked in tune to her howls of pain and indignation. When she was finally allowed up she stood rubbing at her rear cheeks, her face set in a resentful scowl.

'And if you continue to pout you'll get more,' the Baroness warned her, 'with my hairbrush. Now go and feed Aunt Isabella.'

Cicely made a face and continued to rub at her bottom, still defiant.

Florence had watched the spanking with a curious mixture of sympathy and approval, in silence, but now gave a sad shake of her head and spoke up. 'Run along, Cicely, or it will be the cane.'

Not deigning to answer, Cicely gave an angry toss of her unruly curls and stamped indoors, but Florence's argument had been persuasive. Being spanked across the knee was something she could cope with, but the cane was another matter entirely, although having given in didn't make the task in front of her any easier. She climbed the stairs slowly, twice stopping as some new argument occurred to her, but both grounded on the fact that if she employed them she was more than likely to end up touching her toes with her bare bottom sticking out of her drawers as she was given six of the best.

She hesitated again when she reached the landing. Aunt Isabella's door was closed and there was absolute silence, which was only to be expected. Plucking up her courage, she went in, taking a moment for her eyes to adapt to the dull orange light of the single candle that illuminated the room. In front of her was a great four-poster bed, the canopy half-concealing the occupant, who lay with the bed sheets pulled back, her body limp and naked, the skin stretched taut and yellow over angular bones, the eyes sunk deep in their sockets, the mass of ghost-pale hair oddly incongruous.

'Aunt Isabella?' Cicely queried, suddenly worried that the woman on the bed might actually be dead.

A voice like cobweb answered her. 'Cicely? Come close, my dear.'

Cicely obeyed, seating herself on the bed and extending one cautious hand to touch the desiccated chest. Aunt Isabella's flesh felt cold and oddly waxy, while one withered nipple had already begun to crack, yet the bony hand which had settled across Cicely's shoulders was pulling her in with considerable strength.

'I'm sorry we left you so long,' Cicely said quietly, as she allowed herself to be drawn in against Aunt Isabella's mouth.

A sharp cry of pain escaped Cicely lips as the fangs punctured her neck, and Aunt Isabella had begun to feed. Cicely stayed still, trembling badly, her breathing growing deeper and more urgent as the blood flowed from her neck and into the mouth of the creature suckling from her. The one bony hand had stayed on her back and the other now moved up, slowly, to scrabble at the front of Cicely's corset.

'Please, not yet,' she sighed.

She was ignored, her corset tugged down to spill out her breasts, while fingers like claws scraped across the soft flesh. A rasping groan escaped Aunt Isabella's throat as she continued to feed, with Cicely now sobbing in her grip. She'd shut her eyes tight, unable to watch, for all that she knew exactly what was happening, and no longer able to escape had she wanted to, with her body held tight in a bony embrace and Aunt Isabella's long, curved fangs pushed deep into her neck.

Even when the emaciated hand released her breasts to move lower, Cicely stayed as she was, whimpering faintly into Aunt Isabella's abundant hair as long, thin fingers pushed in at the slit of her drawers. She cried out as what felt like gristle touched her cunt, but her thighs had come wide, seemingly of their own accord, to allow one slender digit inside her. Now penetrated, her sobs grew deeper, more urgent, and still the blood flowed.

Cicely gave in, letting her thighs open wider still and throwing her head back, her neck fully exposed as Aunt Isabella climbed on to her. Pinned down on the bed, with the fangs locked into her flesh as now strong fingers worked in her cunt, Cicely found herself helpless, unable to resist either mentally or physically as she gave strength to her aunt. Her heart was pumping fast, her breath coming in urgent, ragged gasps that broke to an involuntary cry of ecstasy as she came to orgasm under the now firm and pliant fingers.

A moment later Aunt Isabella pulled back, and for a long while the two women lay together in silence.

Only when the gashes in Cicely's neck had fully healed did she voice her feelings. 'I do wish you wouldn't masturbate me while you feed. It's most unsettling.'

'It makes your heart beat faster and improves the flow of blood,' Aunt Isabella replied. 'As I believe I have explained before. And, besides, you whimper so nicely.'

Cicely made a face but didn't reply. Aunt Isabella was now propped up in her bed, her round, pale limbs still naked, but smooth and supple, her breasts full and firm, her belly a gentle womanly curve. She had fed well, rather better than usual, which had left Cicely feeling weak and a little dizzy.

'I see you're dressed for town,' Aunt Isabella said after a while. 'New blood?'

'I hope so,' Cicely replied. 'There's a club I want to try, full of boys who think they're vampires, girls too.'

Aunt Isabella gave a wistful sigh, then spoke again. 'You couldn't bring one back this time, could you? A girl, of course.'

'You know I can't, Auntie,' Cicely replied. 'That sort of thing gets noticed nowadays, and we couldn't very well let her go afterwards, not with the way Florence looks, and … and you.'

'But I'm beautiful,' Aunt Isabella protested.

She had risen from the bed, her naked milk-white flesh glimmering in the candlelight, her hair a cascade of pure

28

silver, her eyes flickering with reflections of vivid red. Her mouth was now full, her lips a delicate blushing mauve, the fangs that rose both up and down from her jaws long and sharp.

'Beautiful,' Cicely agreed, 'and very obviously a vampire, a real vampire.'

'Oh, I don't know,' Aunt Isabella replied, 'only the other day you were saying how good the make-up is these days, and that film, *Van Helsing*, was most convincing, I thought.'

'It's called CGI, Auntie,' Cicely said patiently. 'Computer-generated imagery. It's not real.'

Aunt Isabella was making a critical inspection of one heavy white breast and didn't reply immediately.

'I must go,' Cicely stated.

'Flawless,' Aunt Isabella remarked, 'the colour and texture of cream as one sweet boy once remarked.'

'Did he live?'

'No.'

'They don't often, do they? Not with you.'

'I can't help it if I have a passionate nature.'

'Maybe not, but that is another very good reason for you not to come out with me tonight.'

'Oh very well, give your auntie a kiss then, and you'd better run along.'

Cicely stood to kiss her aunt, their lips meeting in a faint caress, only to open in passion, their mouths wide together, tongues entwined, with no sound but the faint chink of their fangs.

'Little and pointy in the mouth, and such big boobies,' Aunt Isabella remarked as she finally pulled away. 'You're a lucky girl, Cicely.'

Cicely smiled and kissed her aunt once more before scampering from the room, only to slow as she reached the top of the stairs. She'd let Aunt Isabella take more blood than usual, while it had been a long time since she'd fed herself. Her need was now urgent, but she found herself obliged to support herself on the banister as she descended the stairs and she tripped on the last step as she came back out into the moonlit garden.

'Are you all right, my dear?' Florence asked.

'She was a little greedy,' Cicely answered.

'You really must learn to assert yourself,' the Baroness advised. 'Don't put up with her nonsense.'

'I just need to sit down for a moment,' Cicely said. 'Then I'd better go.'

'You're weak,' the Baroness stated. 'I shall come with you.'

'Come with me?' Cicely said in surprise. 'But, Baroness, you haven't left the grounds in years. Decades in fact.'

'Since 1952, to be precise,' the Baroness responded.

'Really, my dear,' Florence put in. 'I'm not at all sure that it's a good idea.'

'Nonsense,' the Baroness answered her. 'It will do me good.'

'Things have changed,' Cicely said.

'I have seen change across very nearly two hundred years, Cicely St Cyr,' the Baroness pointed out. 'And now I am of a mind to see some more. Besides, you are so weak you can barely stand.'

'I can manage, thank you.'

'Not another word, Cicely. Let us go to the carriage.'

'The car, Baroness,' Cicely pointed out. 'I drive a car.'

'A most vulgar abbreviation, and a most vulgar vehicle. Blood-red paintwork indeed. Sometimes your sense of humour is positively grotesque.'

'It's inconspicuous. Speaking of which, at the very least you will have to change.'

'Certainly not!'

The Baroness had risen and stalked into the house. Cicely made to follow, but Florence spoke up. 'Shall I come too, my dear?'

Cicely turned to make a brief inspection of the corpse-white face, the ragged grave shroud that only partially concealed the emaciated body, the inch-long fangs projecting over bloodless lips. 'I'm not sure it would be your thing,' she said.

'Perhaps not,' Florence agreed.

Cicely followed the Baroness through the house, throwing on a coat as she went, then out to the stable

31

yard, where a double row of vacant stalls faced each other across time-worn flagstones. Her car stood to one side, the colour just evident under the brilliant moon.

'And why so small?' the Baroness demanded, picking up the conversation more or less where she'd left off. 'A carriage should reflect a lady's status. I had a beautiful black and gold landau once, drawn by a team of six greys ...'

The Baroness continued her reminiscences, as Cicely started the car and drove out from the stable block and down the long curving avenue of intertwined beeches that hid the house from any curious gaze. Another mile and she was on the motorway, with her companion now silent as she watched the passing scenery and speaking only when they had stopped near to the old warehouse in which the club was being held. A sign in glaring red-orange neon above the doors proclaimed the name of the premises 'Suzi's', while a painted board advertised the fetish vamp night that had drawn Cicely's attention.

'Rather common, is it not?' the Baroness remarked as she climbed from the car. 'But you're sensible, of course. Nobody notices the occasional missing peasant, after all, but take somebody from even a moderately notable family and, oh, the fuss!'

'I think it might be better if you didn't refer to them as peasants,' Cicely suggested.

'But they are peasants,' the Baroness pointed out as

she made a disdainful inspection of a group of girls in nothing but fishnet tights and brightly coloured under-wear, 'although in my day –'

'Oh shut up!' Cicely said.

The Baroness gave her a haughty look but made no move towards reprisal. Neither drew comment at the door, where Cicely paid for two tickets, admitting them to a great square of open space, flickering with coloured lights and loud with music. The floor was already crowded, with dancers sporting a vast variety of styles: dour or flamboyant Goths in their black finery, role players and cosplayers, dominants and submissives, fetishists of every description.

'Extraordinary!' the Baroness remarked, her voice raised above the music. 'Although I recall a ball at Chantilly, given by the last Condé …'

Cicely was not listening, but concentrating on the hunt. Some three hundred people were visible, one of whom would be giving up his, or her, blood, maybe more than one, especially if the Baroness chose to join the chase. It was never an easy choice, but always a thrilling one, while the occasional rejection only added to her hunger. The victim had to be pretty, fey and sufficiently dedicated to the vampire cult to allow Cicely to feed as they made love, something the presence of the Baroness made rather awkward.

'Do you think, perhaps –' she began, only to break

off as she turned to discover that her companion was no longer with her. 'Bother!'

Irritated, Cicely went in search of the Baroness, a task made harder by the jumping shadows and because well over half the guests at the club were dressed entirely in black. Climbing to a balcony, she scanned the throng in the main room over and again before moving on to the bar, then into a series of smaller rooms set aside for more intimate encounters. She found the Baroness in the very last, the darkest, the deepest within the labyrinthine warehouse, and what she saw made her gape in astonishment.

The room had been fitted out as if it were a medieval dungeon, with walls painted to resemble dripping grey-green stone and a single high window set with rusting iron bars. Against the far wall was a tall cross of heavy beams fitted with chains and leather straps, while other pieces of furniture intended to aid in restraint and punishment stood to the sides. A man was strapped to the cross, naked, his burly back and heavy buttocks criss-crossed with scarlet welts, while three others knelt on the floor, their faces pressed to the dirty concrete. Between them stood the Baroness, her thin lips set in a pleased smile as she employed a long single-tail whip with practised efficiency.

'Ah, there you are, my dear,' the Baroness said when she finally noticed Cicely. 'I must say, this is tremendous fun! I had no idea modern people knew their place so well.'

'They –' Cicely began and thought better of it, breaking off as one of the men on the floor spoke up, addressing the Baroness.

'Mistress, please, I beg you, just one kiss of your boots. I'll do anything you want, anything you say!'

'I want to please you, Mistress,' another said, looking up with an expression of awe. 'Make me your slave, Mistress, I beg you. I have no limits. You can do anything to me, anything!'

'You see,' the Baroness remarked to Cicely, 'positively servile! Is it usually like this?'

'Not for me,' Cicely admitted, as the Baroness extended one booted foot from beneath her skirts to allow the man who'd asked the favour to plant a single kiss on the toe.

'They recognise nobility, of course,' the Baroness said as she began to flick her whip at the man on the cross, aiming between his legs to snap at the dangling testicles, 'but, really, I haven't had so much fun in years. You, peasant, you bleed well. My friend is a vampire. Let her feed.'

The man she'd addressed looked up doubtfully, his eyes moving first to the Baroness and then to Cicely, or, more precisely, to her chest. 'Er ...' he began. 'That's not really my thing.'

'Um ...' Cicely put in, but the man clearly assumed she was a role player.

'You said you wished to serve me, did you not?' the

Baroness stated. 'You said you would do anything to please me. Look on it as a test of your devotion.'

'Yes, Mistress, but –' the man began, only to be interrupted by another.

'Your slut may feed from me, Mistress. I would be honoured.'

'Slut?' Cicely queried, but the man had already been sent in her direction with a well-aimed kick of the Baroness' boot.

He stayed down, his head hung to the floor, exposing his neck, a sight too enticing to allow Cicely to hold back. She would have preferred a girl, or a younger, more virile man, but the victim she had been offered was well fed and sleek, which promised rich, nourishing blood, while it was impossible to deny that his craven submission had fired her lust. Sinking down, she took a firm hold across his back, pressed her open mouth to his neck and sank her fangs deep into his resilient flesh.

'Jesus shit!' he squealed, and tried to rise, but too late. Cicely had him in her grip, too strong for any mere mortal to break, with her fangs sunk in deep and the blood already flowing into her mouth. As she'd hoped, it was thick and rich, sending her dizzy with pleasure as she swallowed and swallowed again, breaking off only with an effort. The man rolled back as she released her grip, to stare up at her, wide-eyed with horror, his gaze fixed to her open, bloody mouth as she wiped away a trickle of blood.

'You fucking weirdo!' he swore, and he scrabbled to his feet and fled the room.

'He'll report us,' Cicely said.

'You were only playing,' the Baroness said blithely, 'and, if we can whip them, why can't we bite them? Tell me that, Miss Cicely St Cyr?'

'True,' Cicely admitted, 'but please could you let me choose the next one? There's a knack to this.'

'Make me your next victim, I beg you, Mistress,' a voice sounded at Cicely's shoulder. 'I am worthy, Mistress.'

She hadn't looked back since entering the room, and was surprised to find a knot of male faces peering in from the gloom beyond the door. The man who'd spoken was the largest of them, tall and well built, his great barrel chest and tree-trunk legs naked, his crotch concealed only by a straining pouch of thin black rubber.

'Do you mean that?' she asked, opening her mouth to show her fangs and the bloody interior. 'I bite.'

'Please, yes,' he begged, his voice weak with need, although others in the audience were more critical, one giving his opinion that Cicely's fangs were obviously fake and another suggesting that her image would be more effective if both her breasts hadn't popped free of her corset as she fed.

Cicely ignored them as she beckoned her victim closer. The situation was ideal, a fine, big young man to feed on and a disbelieving audience, which would allow both her and the Baroness to gorge themselves to satiation. He was as good as his promise too, coming into the room to wait patiently as Cicely released the man on the cross. Both the other men had fled, allowing them to work uninterrupted save for the occasional comment from the door.

Whichever of the men had originally owned the whip had lacked the courage to retrieve it, allowing the Baroness to liven up their new victim with a few smart cuts to his legs and chest, while Cicely fixed his ankle cuffs into place. He seemed already in ecstasy, moaning as the leather smacked down across his flesh, and as the Baroness stepped close the look he gave her showed no fear, only adoration.

'Let us see then,' she said gently. 'Are you truly worthy?'

He gave a low whimper in response as her lips brushed his neck, then a sharp cry of pain as her fangs went home. Her eyes closed in bliss as she began to drink, while Cicely looked on with a quiet smile to see her friend and mentor indulging herself for the first time in so very long. For a while she simply watched as the Baroness fed, her own belly already round with blood, but with Florence and Aunt Isabella to feed as well she had soon moved close, only not to the man's neck, but to his crotch.

It was a rare treat, one she hadn't allowed herself in

a while, and she smacked her lips in anticipation as she pulled their victim's rubber pants low to free a large, heavily hooded cock straight into her mouth. He groaned as Cicely began to suck, as helpless to the pleasure of being in her mouth as had he not been restrained, while even the crowd at the door had gone silent. Another tug at his pants and his balls were free, allowing her to lick at the salty flesh before taking his now stiff cock into her mouth once more. Her hands went to her breasts, stroking herself as she sucked, now dizzy with reaction to the long thick cock shaft in her mouth. He began to push, fucking her lips, and she slid a hand into the slit of her drawers, masturbating shamelessly for the sheer joy of sucking his cock, and brought herself to climax at the exact instant he gave her what she wanted most of all, a warm, sticky mouthful of come.

Cicely swallowed and rocked back on her heels, smiling happily for what she'd done. Above her, the Baroness was still feeding, with a long trickle of blood running down over the man's shoulder and across his chest. Cicely came up a little, to lap at the deep-red trail, cleaning up the spillage before gently detaching the Baroness from the man's neck.

'Enough, darling. That must be enough.'

Both the man and the Baroness nodded and behind them the watchers broke into applause. The Baroness responded with a carefully measured nod, while Cicely curtsied before setting to work to release the man from his cuffs.

'Thank you, Mistress,' he sighed, 'and you too, Cicely. May I buy you both a drink, because I think I need one. I'm Dave, by the way.'

'Blanche Iodie Marie-Sabine d'Annecy, Baroness de Brouilly, charmed. A cut of champagne would be pleasant.'

* * *

Four hours later Cicely and the Baroness left the club. It had been a good evening, by any standards. The story of their performance in the dungeon had quickly circulated, leaving the Baroness the object of adoring male attention from all sides, while Cicely had been able to feed three more times, to leave her belly swollen with blood and her breasts engorged to the point at which fluid had begun to seep from her nipples.

'I do hope Florence is hungry,' she said as she drew away into the now empty streets.

'Yes,' the Baroness replied vaguely, her mind clearly on other things. 'Ah, what a night! I am not certain I recall a better, and I really had no idea that modern men had such an instinctive ability to recognise their betters.'

Cicely didn't answer, more concerned with her aching breasts and straining belly.

'It is only natural, of course,' the Baroness continued, 'that the lower orders ...'

Bright headlight beams illuminated the interior of the car from behind them, making it difficult for Cicely to see, while she was more than familiar with the Baroness' personal philosophy in any case. Concentrating on her driving and her ever more urgent need to feed one of her friends, she had quickly put everything else from her mind. Only when she was almost at the gates of the house and the car behind them was still close did she wonder if it was following them. She turned on to the drive and the lights swung around behind her.

'Whoever could that be?' the Baroness asked.

'I suspect I know,' Cicely answered her.

She got out of the car, to find Dave already standing by his own, with a hang-dog expression on his face.

'I – I thought ... my Mistress.'

'Go home,' Cicely urged. 'You can't come here, this is where we live.'

'I live only to serve my Mistress,' he replied.

'We could do with a houseboy,' the Baroness spoke from behind.

'No we could not,' Cicely answered firmly.

'I don't see why not,' the Baroness went on. 'It would certainly be a help to have somebody around during the day.'

'Because ... because ... because a thousand things!' Cicely stormed.

'You're being very awkward, Cicely St Cyr,' the Baroness continued. 'You wouldn't want me to have to spank you again, would you?'

'No,' Cicely stated emphatically, 'but –'

'Then be quiet,' the Baroness instructed. 'Come, David, bring your carriage into the stable yard.'

'You can't do this!' Cicely stormed the moment he was safely out of hearing. 'What about Florence and Aunt Isabella!?'

'They are two old ladies in poor health,' the Baroness replied. 'That is all he needs to know.'

'They're milk-white, they have huge fangs. Florence looks as if she's dead, completely, and as for Aunt Isabella!'

They had been walking swiftly down the drive as they spoke, and reached the front of the house to find their companions not inside as they had supposed, but on the lawn, head to toe, locked in passion, tongues feasting on pale cunts, fangs on open display, trickles of blood running down over each other's body.

'Um,' Cicely began, and broke off at the sound of a wet, gurgling noise followed by a dull thud from behind them.

Dave lay on the ground, unconscious. Cicely ducked down to take his pulse.

'Is he alive?' the Baroness asked.

'Yes,' Cicely answered.

'Oh dear, did you bring a young man back?' Florence queried.

'My, he's a big one,' Aunt Isabella put in.

Dave's eyes flickered open, to take in the four women looking down on him, then closed again.

'We're going to have to keep him now,' the Baroness said, 'and think of the advantages.'

Cicely drew a heavy sigh. 'OK, OK, I'll chain him in the cellar. After all, a girl's got to eat.'

Crystal
Primula Bond

There was no air in the cells and I wriggled on the hard chair. My armpits prickled uncomfortably and my white shirt felt too tight as if the buttons might burst off.

I was in heaven, and also in hell. Heaven, because I was working with the barrister of my dreams. Hell, because also in this tiny room was a nasty piece of work called Al Drake who was accused of attempting to murder his girlfriend.

'Getting instructions will be like getting blood out of a stone,' muttered my boss that morning, handing me the file. 'But Marcus Scott is the best man for the job.'

Al Drake had a frozen, pock-marked face and colourless, icy eyes, and those eyes were fixed on the straining top button of my shirt, where my breasts thumped heavily. The silence was toxic. Marcus was leaning across the table with his fingers joined in a church steeple, waiting for the answer to his last question.

'It's not guilty, because she asked me to do it.' Al's voice rasped like rusty hinges.

Marcus dropped his hands. 'The victim *asked* you to slash at her jugular?'

'Not with a weapon.' Al shook his head, and there was a curious waft of sweet lavender. 'I bit her.'

Marcus opened the file of photographs. Two arrows of blood running down a long white neck, staining a lacy dress ripped off one shoulder.

'That was not inflicted by human teeth,' said Marcus. 'We have to find the knife, Al. The neighbour saw you standing over her, all that blood, Crystal unconscious –'

'He's enjoying this, isn't he? *All that blood*.' Al was addressing me, eyes raking over my face, my breasts, my legs.

Instead of being repulsed my stomach twisted sharply, answering his lust.

'We need to enter your plea today,' Marcus persisted.

'You seen my Crystal recently?' Al hissed. 'Absolutely no scar.' His lips peeled back showing sharp white canines. 'A lovely neck, just like Virginie's here.'

'How do you know my name?'

Now Marcus glanced at my neck, a flush rising in his cheek. The crazy pulse would give my crush away, surely. 'We'll need a psychiatrist's report.'

'So examine her, not me.' Al rapped at the door. 'She's enthralled with her new life. Soon as this crap is over, she wants me home for a good fucking.'

My top button broke free and my shirt fell open. I sat there, temporarily paralysed and whimpering faintly, while both men had a good long look at my breasts, swelling like dough, nipples poking urgently against the satin cups. And both men smiled.

* * *

A group of grisly vampires whooped through the dark as I left the court. Reminding me I had nothing to wear for Janie's Halloween party. But like an answer to a prayer there was a new pop-up shop across the alleyway. Beneath the Gothic swirly signage the bright window was riotous. Headless mannequins in strapless ball gowns posed with diamante tiaras circling their wooden necks, as if the head where the tiara once perched had been guillotined.

Inside, the shop was a mist of sandalwood, patchouli and more lavender. Music twanged hypnotically. A flock of boas feathered me as I paused before a rail of antique lace dresses, swaying as if other fingers had just brushed them.

'Can I help you?'

A seated woman was knitting what looked like a cobweb. Her face was very white, her mouth a red slash and she was wearing an Edwardian blouse with a high ruffled neck. I'd seen her before.

'Lovely things you have here,' I said, fingering the dresses.

'Vintage treasures. All with their own bloody history.' The corner of her red mouth twitched.

The door jingled open. The dresses rippled as if in greeting.

'You shall go to the ball, Cinderella,' said Marcus. He was the same height as the mahogany grandfather clock positioned like a sentry by the door. Suddenly there was the same suffocating claustrophobia I'd felt in the cells.

The woman hovered up behind me, holding one of the dresses. She was as flimsy as the dress itself. But Marcus paled as if he'd seen a ghost.

'Try this on,' she murmured, pulling me with surprising strength between the cupboards and shelves to the back.

We stood in front of a tarnished mirror and my coat and blouse came off, her stiff cold fingers making cool stripes on my skin as she helped me undress. She fastened my hair up with a single knitting needle, unzipped my skirt, eased the dress over my hips, but paused as the antique lace tried to make sense of my modern curves.

'I've seen you before,' I murmured, as her black eyes glittered.

'Oh, I don't think so.' She stroked my ribs gently, the lace dangling like a rag from her hand. Her fingers closed over them like white spiders. I gasped. She was close, her long body pressing along mine. 'You're all new.'

The cubicle curtain wafted. Marcus was still prowling about outside.

'Marcus, wait for me!' I called. 'You can walk me to the tube.'

He cleared his throat. 'Do you mind telling me where all this stock comes from?'

'Why, do you think it's off the back of a lorry?' I started to laugh, but the woman, still stroking my breasts and starting to squeeze now, answered him calmly enough.

'My partner is indisposed at the moment so he has me travelling all over the world, collecting things. But mostly it comes from Transylvania.' Her voice was thin as a reed.

'Ooh.' I demonstrated an exaggerated shiver. 'That's where Dracula lives, isn't it?'

On the other side of the curtain Marcus gave an evil laugh, like a pantomime villain.

The woman shrugged wearily. She looked as if the life was draining out of her. Her eyes were dark like beads of jet, fixed on me in the mirror. I bit my lip, but too hard. There was the quick metallic tang of my own blood. Time to go. I started to turn, but the woman tightened her grip on me, her nostrils flaring, and she started to stroke her long fingers across my nipples. She smiled, teeth glinting between her red lips slashing open her white face. She looked hollow, like a Russian doll, positively sickly in fact, yet her fingers were strong, and insistent, and I was beginning to breathe faster as she stroked my nipples up into points, and started moving her body against me, her bony hips against my bottom, her small breasts, hidden under the Edwardian blouse, pushing against my spine.

Her hands slid down, pushing my knickers down over my buttocks, stroked my bottom, came up again and unclipped my bra. I gasped again as my breasts thumped softly into her waiting hands, the nipples shrinking into stiff points. A ball of lust rolled in my stomach as the woman moulded my breasts in her palms, each forefinger circling each raspberry nipple.

'Virginie? You OK in there?'

Marcus was fidgeting outside the cubicle.

'Yeees,' I moaned in answer, and he whisked the curtain aside. I couldn't look at his face. I couldn't move. My legs were shaking. Dark desire lurched in me as the woman calmly continued pinching my nipples, smiling over my shoulder in the mirror as her white fingers started treading down my stomach. I could feel her breath shivering on my neck.

'That dress will be fine for the party,' Marcus said to her. 'But we need to go now.'

'When the clock strikes I'll have her ready,' murmured the woman, walking her fingers right down to my pussy, the neat row of hair curling up with damp excitement. I tried to make sense of what they were saying, but I was dizzy with the heat, the thick perfume in the shop, this woman's fingers, and Marcus almost guarding us.

My thighs parted eagerly, even though my legs were still shaking. Her fingers paused, then tiptoed into my hidden crack, sliding down then whisking up again.

I was powerless now, staring at our reflection, at Marcus' eyes, blacker than ever and strangely expressionless, lasering through me. The woman's eyes fluttered closed. She moved her fingers rhythmically inside my pussy, the friction making my tender parts sing, and then she dipped her head, her sparkling earrings swinging against my cheek. Her lips brushed my neck. I flinched because it tickled, but the coolness of her breath and the dampness of her lips made it a grown-up tickle. A caress. It felt as if ice was crystallising under her lips, but her quick panting was like a dying kitten. She obviously sensed my deepening pleasure, because she moved her mouth gently round to the side, under my ear.

'Get her ready. Now,' Marcus rasped into the perfumed silence. The dim lamplight made his eyes glow red now, like coals. 'Virginie, concentrate!'

I couldn't move, despite the order in his voice. Concentrate on what? Buying the dress and getting out? I had no idea what he was talking about. And the woman was ignoring him, and I was stuck on her fingers buried inside my cunt, working relentlessly, thumb playing over my burning clit, all distracting me from rational thought, drawing me onwards as I got weaker and weaker, trembling with approaching ecstasy.

The woman swayed slightly as if she was going to faint, but started kissing my neck, licking it and sucking at it. I'd never really been kissed there before. Not one of my favourite zones because I don't like the tickling. But the response on my skin had changed from tickle to tingle, and reached deeper. She was nibbling at me, as if she wanted to eat me, but delicately, like a bird, her fingers strong inside me, her body pressed hard up against me, then as her teeth started to nip at my neck we started to sway together as if in a strange *pas de deux*.

As my cunt started to suck at her fingers and I jerked against her hand, desperate to come, my head felt severed from reality, like those mannequins in the window. The grandfather clock by the door wheezed, whirred and started to chime like Big Ben. The shop seemed to shrink, the displays and hangers sliding inwards, then the walls, everything started to spin lazily as the woman grazed and bit harder into my neck, the sharp jabbing pain radiating into quick, hot pleasure. It seemed to echo what was happening between my legs, and now there was a high-pitched singing and whispering of voices and the frantic pulsing of my blood in my ears.

Marcus seemed to waver like a candle flame, then split into two as I tried to focus on his grinning face but then everything splintered as I juddered to climax, shaking, trembling, my legs giving way, the woman holding me up and really biting into me now, as if I were a tasty morsel, and she was moaning quietly now, as I realised I was, too, and all at once there was a sickening popping sensation which caused a shower of stars to explode inside my skull as her teeth actually pierced through my skin and I felt the blood spurt angrily from my neck, strong and hot, and I just had time to see it in the mirror, beading on my neck, red on white, dripping down over the woman's chin and lacing through her fingers which had come up to my shoulders, before the lights went out and I fainted dead away.

* * *

'Virginie! Virginie!'

I opened my eyes, expecting to be lying on the floor of the shop, but I was walking, fully clothed, along a pot-holed pavement towards a tall townhouse. Curiously, there was no traffic, although I thought I heard the clip-clop of horses' hooves from another street.

It was pitch dark out here, no street lights, no lights from the other houses, not even a moon. I had no idea where I was. But I wasn't afraid. Quite the opposite. I was buzzing with energy and euphoria as hidden forces dragged me towards the house. The door was open, leading the way into a hallway and staircase all lit up with fairy lights and carved pumpkins. There were witches, wizards, frogs, skeletons and fairies wandering around with huge goblets of champagne or dancing wildly to heavy music playing further inside. Nailed to the walls were enormous glass cases full of black butterflies, beetles and scorpions.

'The vestal virgin. Look at you!'

Marcus, dressed now as a highwayman in a frilly white shirt and black eye mask, welcomed me with open arms, as if this was his party. He pulled me inside. A woman in a white dress moved close beside me, and when I turned I realised I was looking into another mirror. My hair was still twisted up in the knitting needle, but my face had been painted dead white, my lips bright red. There was a pearl choker round my throat, and I was wearing the lacy dress from the shop which clung to me like a second skin yet was cut to fall away from my shoulders, almost away from my breasts, too, as if someone had been ripping it.

'This isn't the right place, Marcus!' I shouted as I was pushed by the crowd of strangers into a kind of ballroom all lit up by flickering sconces. 'I'm supposed to be at my friend Janie's, in Clapham –'

On the far side of the room was a huge glass awning leading out to the dark garden, twined with ivy and brambles, and out on the lawn was a bubbling cauldron where witches spiked lumps of bleeding red meat into their mouths with pitchforks and fake bats swung on invisible strings from the trees. The moon had come out, red as if it was bleeding, glowing between the shredded clouds which streaked the sky like claw marks.

On the far side of the cauldron I saw a man wearing what looked like a death's head mask, but when he waggled a gloved hand I saw that it was no mask, but the unmistakable face of Al Drake.

I tried to scream, but my voice came out garbled, low and guttural, and when I looked again the apparition had gone. I grabbed Marcus, circling him like a panther. I tried to marshal my scattering thoughts. 'I've got to get out of here!'

Marcus laughed his pantomime laugh. 'It's Halloween, V! Everyone wears masks! Your friend will never know if you're there or not. This is where you're destined to be.'

'I can't be bothered to slog all the way to Clapham, anyway.'

I had never felt so awake. So alert. All that dizziness earlier had gone. I hadn't felt this full and fit and fresh for years. And Marcus looked wired, too, bright-eyed and jumping restlessly from foot to foot.

'Which reminds me,' I cooed, stroking his arm. 'What did you mean in the shop about getting me ready?'

'I wanted her to dress you up like a princess.'

'You said Cinderella, actually. So am I going to turn into a pumpkin at midnight?'

'Not a pumpkin, V. We're way past that now! All the clocks have stopped. So. Don't you like your costume?'

He laughed, and snaked his arm round my waist. That was more like it. A luscious heat snaked through me. It was like I could trace the network of veins through my body, track each pathway and offshoot, feel the river of blood keeping me moving. Keeping me alive. I let him draw me close. 'Now come and meet our hostess.'

A tall creature with black hair coiled up on her head and wearing one of the lace dresses from that shop was standing with her back to us in the middle of the room, a golden flame around which huge menacing moths fluttered. Although the music was deafening, she spun round as if she could hear what Marcus was saying, and her eyes, painted with a kind of shimmering grey shadow that sank them back into her head, narrowed into red-glowing slits.

It was the woman from the shop.

'Where have I seen her before, Marcus? Before the shop, I mean?'

He didn't answer. I saw the fire burning in his eyes and jealousy shafted through me. Something had happened between them while I was out cold. Maybe she'd drugged me. Either way she looked different. A few minutes ago she'd looked half-dead, chalk-white and clammy, while she finger-fucked me and nibbled at my skin, sucked on my blood, as if her life depended on it. Now there was a spring in her step, a hectic redness on each cheek, a shine on her lips that wasn't just the blood-red lipstick.

She waved her hand dismissively at a hook-nosed hobgoblin who was trying to talk to her, her nose angled at the creature as if she'd rather stamp on it. Then she stalked towards us, people falling away to let her through like so many autumn leaves.

'I see you've brought my twin. How kinky is that?' She drifted up to us. She was indeed wearing the exact same dress as mine, and her black hair was coiled in the same style as mine. Like me, she wore a pearl choker. She held out a tray of burned-looking canapés. 'Devils on horseback?'

She paused as if she'd never seen me before. Then she kissed me full on the lips. I kissed her back, feeling the catlike flick of her wet tongue, before she pulled sharply away and flattened her hand brazenly over Marcus' velvet crotch.

'I'll leave you to it,' I stammered, trying to find my way out of the crowd, but everyone was dancing like there was no tomorrow, arms and legs flailing, faces looming and receding like marionettes, some retreating to the sofas at the side of the room, some, oh my God, grabbing at each other's clothes, ripping off dresses and trousers, knickerbockers and camisoles, white legs, everyone so white, white arms, white faces bending into each other, kissing, licking, biting. Everyone biting, on the neck. Everyone, I noticed with a kick in my stomach, opening their mouths when they went in for the kill, lips folding back over sharp white teeth.

I moved through the crowd, feet barely touching the floor, was tossed and manhandled, hands and fingers on me, lips and teeth, and then I saw a beautiful young man cowering in the corner, dressed in a pure white toga. He had golden curls under a laurel wreath.

I glided towards him with my newfound gracefulness. Sat on the arm of the gilded armchair. Leaned myself against him.

'Wrong party, honey?' I purred. 'You look far too pure and innocent to be out with the ghoulies and ghosties. And something tells me this is going to turn into an orgy.'

There was a rasp in my voice I didn't recognise, but it must have sounded sexy because the guy looked up and smiled.

'I always dress like this at parties. And I always manage to cut myself. God knows what Marcus will say when he sees I've broken one of his precious Romanian goblets.'

Glass was shattered on the floor, and he was holding his finger scored across with a neat red line where blood was beginning to bubble along its seam.

I took his finger and put it into my mouth, licking round it oh so suggestively, then sucking, drinking in the foreign taste of his blood, smearing it round my lips, then I lifted his chin up and started to kiss him, slow pushes of my tongue between his teeth, his hesitation, then he pulled me over on to his lap so that I was straddling him, the lace dress floating up my legs, straddling his golden bare thighs, feeling the hardness of his prick under the stupid toga.

I was so restless, though. Normally kissing a gorgeous boy at a party would be enough for me – the attention, the kissing, the easy path to seduction– but I couldn't rest with the taste of his blood still on my tongue. So, hooking my leg round his bare thigh, I nuzzled into his muscled neck where his pulse throbbed anxiously like a trapped animal. I sucked the skin up hard between my red lips, and sank my teeth through the resisting skin, felt that same pop but this time it was in my teeth, not in my head, and there was a jet of hot blood, thick and heady like wine, shooting straight down my throat like spunk, making a splattering necklace of droplets round his perfect white toga, making him sink to the floor like a rag doll.

I stood over him for a long time, noticing for the first time the two red marks on everyone's necks as they came close to us and danced away again. I watched as the boy's breathing returned, until his eyes snapped open, fiery with life. My body soared with an avalanche of ice, rushing through the branches and tributaries of my veins, singing in my ears, unveiling my eyes. The closer the air, the heavier the perfume; the cold, despite the roaring of my blood, prickled my skin. Everyone in the room felt the same. Wild, hungry lust, thirst, greed, all the deadly sins. I could see everything clear as crystal, spot lit, sharply outlined, brightly lit. I could have any one of these crazy people. But I wanted Marcus.

The house seemed to rise forever but I flew right to the top to find, sitting on narrow steps leading to the attic, the shop woman. She was leaning back on her elbows, her legs open, her curiously bushy crotch on display, one finger in her mouth, the other hand spreading herself open.

'Now that I've had my way with Marcus, do you want to carry on where we left off?'

Her voice was a hypnotic kitteny hiss. I knelt obediently down on the step and pushed my face between her thighs, held them open with my hands, and inhaled that musky lavender scent again. I was about to lick her when male hands pulled my buttocks open and the cool, smooth shape of a hard cock nudged at my cunt, nosed over my clit.

'Marcus! Join the party, darling,' purred the woman to my invisible lover. 'We haven't much time.'

I tipped my bottom in the air as I bent to lick her, and felt the cock edging right into me now, deeper and deeper, pulling out a little to tease me, then in again, just as my tongue was sliding into her, getting rougher the further he plunged so that my legs turned to jelly and spirals of hot desire twisted inside me. He started to fuck me, throwing me forwards, and I must have nipped her tender flesh because she gave a kind of unearthly howl as the blood smeared my tongue, so I licked faster, and Marcus fucked harder, our voices all jagged and sharp as I licked her to a frenzy and he came inside me and my own body milked him for every drop of the white stuff.

Somewhere a cockerel crew, and the woman slithered away.

'I must go to Al,' I thought she said.

She was gone, shedding the dress like a skin.

Marcus turned me round. 'You can't go home now, Virginie. There's no time.'

The dawn must have been breaking through the dusty attic windows because a finger of light was crawling down the steps. Marcus rushed me through the quiet, deserted house, muttering and whimpering. He dragged me into a bedroom festooned with dustsheets and cobwebs and slammed the door.

'Where are you, Marcus?' I whispered, but there was no answer. Understanding nothing, I wrenched open the shutters to break the choking darkness, and as the dawn blossomed across my face I just had time, before the sunlight dissolved me, little by little, to see the Gothic swirling writing sewn into the woman's discarded dress and, I knew, in mine.

And it read *Crystal*.

Mist
Noelle Keely

I lay alone on the bed in the locked bedroom. It was after eight o'clock and the world outside my tiny window was dark. Edward worked nights, so my time of relative peace and safety was also the night. I was hungry – he left me water, but I'd been allowed to bring only an apple upstairs with me, and that was long gone. The window opened only a crack, and it was too small to crawl out, even if I'd broken it. I could have yelled for help, but I had little faith in the neighbours. If no one in the neighbourhood had called the police the night I'd almost got away – the night Edward wound up nearly killing me – they wouldn't call the police now.

As I often did, I enumerated ways I could kill myself. Break the too-small window and slit my wrists or stab myself with the shattered glass. Hang myself with a sheet. Swallow some random object and choke, I supposed.

And, as I always did, I chose to live. As long as I was still alive, there was a chance things would change, that his vigilance might slip, that I might be able to get to the city and find a safe house for battered women, that Edward might get hit on the head and jarred into sanity, that someone might finally remember that I existed and come looking for me.

My current life was hellish, but I wasn't ready to die. I remembered wind in my face, and soft grass under my feet, and people who loved me, and steak with a buttery baked potato, and chocolate, and sex that was actually unambiguously fun. As long as I stayed alive, there was a chance I could experience such things again.

Then mist began creeping through the open window.

I didn't bother closing the window. My life was long stretches of boredom interspersed with short bursts of blood, and, while I appreciated the boredom by comparison, I welcomed any distraction, even something as minor as fog. At least the mist was something different from the two-year-old cooking magazine I was reading for the hundredth time, different from the familiar room in which I'd been locked, unless Edward was home to watch me, since my last escape attempt.

The mist felt pleasant against my skin, not cold and dank as I would have expected. At first it brushed my skin gently and uniformly, a cool and comforting caress against the unwelcome nakedness I had to maintain at the moment, since Edward's most recent whim was hiding what few clothes he allowed me to own.

To keep what little sanity I still had, I'd learned to relish what small pleasures came my way: the texture of soft flannel sheets in winter and crisp cotton ones in summer, the taste of food, classical music on the radio. So I revelled in the mist, embracing its novelty.

The mist changed so gradually I wasn't aware at first. From an impersonal natural phenomenon, it took on weight and direction. Its light touch, which started out on all my skin at once, focused its attention on more sensitive areas: my face, my breasts, not the nipples so much as the underside and the valley between them, my throat, the exquisitely ticklish stretch along my collarbone. It felt like lips exploring me, arousing me.

I let myself go with the fantasy, picturing a handsome stranger kissing and caressing me. He was dark-haired and dark-eyed, olive-skinned, a complete contrast to Edward's white-blond Nordic good looks that masked his black heart. He, in my fantasy, kissed me in places I yearned to be kissed, the places a man intent on tender seduction might kiss.

Wrapped in the fantasy – it felt real, but I kept reminding myself it was a fantasy – I moaned and stirred on the bed, wet as I hadn't been since Edward was sure he had isolated me from everyone who had once been close and began to reveal the monster under his sexy mask.

I opened myself to the daydream, to pleasures that felt more real than my bruise-and-blood reality. Edward had taken almost everything else from me, but not this. He'd done his damnedest, over the years, to mould me so I thought only what he wanted me to think. I'd learned to pretend it had worked; it was safer that way. Still some part of me remained free, hidden from his scrutiny. It was that part I let loose now.

Or maybe I was finally losing my grip. If so, there were worse fates than this flavour of madness.

I felt lips, a man's lips, with a moustache that rasped a bit, on my nipple.

It seemed so real, hot and wet. Suckling lips and licking tongue, drawing me deeper in. I gasped and arched up, meeting him – even though he wasn't there.

Imagination. It had to be my imagination, running away with me in my loneliness. It had been a long time since I let my imagination wander down such sensual, dangerous paths. Edward's touch had once been pleasurable. Worse, it still could be, causing me to let down my guard so the pain, when it came, as it always did, was even more shocking. It had been safer for a long time now to cut off my sensual side. It was, as Edward sometimes reminded me, my own fault I was his prisoner, the fault of the sluttiness that tempted me to elope with a much older man at seventeen.

'No,' I heard distinctly. 'Your desire drew me to you. Your desire, and your will to live, can save you.'

The voice I heard was male, deep and lovely and accented – French, I thought. I was pretty sure the voices in my head, if I was going to start hearing them, would sound more like my own inner voice, not so startlingly different from anyone I'd ever known.

'Who are you?' I demanded, then, 'Where are you?'

I suppose I should have been frightened, but the shape of my life was such that an unseen stranger seemed more curious than terrifying. The familiar was terrifying. Something this odd might turn out to be good, even if it was a sign I was delusional. Insane but pleasant delusions would be at least a part-time exit from Edward's world.

'Don't worry about that right now, Carrie. For now, just feel and enjoy.'

The voice came from the mist, diffuse but sexy as the mist that was caressing me. I wanted to make sense of it and at the same time I didn't care what was actually going on. If my mind had finally cracked and my madness took the form of a sensual mist with a French accent, I'd take it over my reality any day.

Then my mist-lover did something a man wouldn't have been able to do. Still suckling and licking and biting at my long-neglected nipples, it moved down my body and began licking between my legs.

Even when Edward was seducing me years ago, he never licked my pussy, never kissed and teased my clit. I knew about such things only from high-school whispers and from books I got to read before Edward stopped my trips to the bookstore and the library and I got to read only what he chose for me.

That damp, velvety touch on my clit was beyond anything I'd ever imagined. It was gentle, but it was determined. It wasn't going to take no for an answer, I sensed, but not in the same way Edward wouldn't. Rather than taking brutally despite a no, the sentience behind this tantalising tongue wanted to turn any possible no into an ecstatic yes.

And so it was with me, despite the oddness of the situation, despite the long fear and longer despair that held me back from relaxing into pleasure, despite the aches from my last beating and the bone-deep pain that never left from the miscarriage six months ago. I had every reason in the world not to come, but between that tongue and the mouth on my nipples – oh, lord, make that mouths, because both nipples were being pleasured now – it didn't take long before I was thrashing and crying out with need. Desire filled me until it finally spilled over. I saw light as I came, not the warm light of the sun, but silver moonlight, calm and peaceful, yet compelling.

At the height of my orgasm, my unseen lover bit me on my mound. It was no gentle nip, either, but a searing bite that felt like it would draw blood. Pain was no friend to me, and pain during the height of sexual pleasure should have thrown me out of the moment into a flashback of all the times Edward hurt me while he used me.

Instead, the white-hot shock of the bite blended with the pleasure I was already feeling, pushing me even higher, and the sensation of that soft, skilled mouth and tongue licking and suckling and soothing the throbbing bite triggered an even stronger orgasm.

My eyes fluttered open. Where there had been only mist before, I saw a man of mist – handsome and well built and dressed in what looked like an elegant old-fashioned suit, but translucent and with no colour to him save for red lips and a smear of what might have been blood on his white cheek. A ghost? A hallucination? I didn't much care.

'Sleep, Carrie,' he said, in that mellifluous French voice, 'and when you wake you'll find the door unlocked.' He gestured with a misty hand.

I felt my consciousness slide away, sending me to warm, welcoming darkness more profound than the darkness in my room.

When I opened my eyes, I was alone in a dishevelled bed, wet between my legs and with a bloodied bruise on my mound, hidden by the dark curls there.

It had been real, then, not just a dream or waking fantasy born of loneliness. Real. Mist had become a man and made love to me.

That meant the door was open. I couldn't move towards it, though. I couldn't bring myself to take those few steps, then put my hand on the door knob. I was trapped by memories of what had happened the last time I'd tried to run. And, just as I steeled my nerve to try anyway, Edward's truck rumbled into the driveway.

At least he'd had a good day. Instead of beating me because the bedroom door was open, he just chuckled when he realised I was so well trained I'd stayed put even though he'd 'forgotten' to lock the door.

* * *

For several more nights the French-accented mist paid me court. On the second night, I tasted an unseen delicious cock as I was licked to orgasm. On the third night that unseen cock moved inside my hungry pussy, and an unseen weight, a man's heavy warm weight, pressed me into the bed. Each night ended with my phantom lover biting me until I bled. Each night, the mist looked more like a man of mist, growing more distinct after he bit me.

On the fourth night, what I saw, lapping blood from a small wound in my inner thigh, was a handsome man, dark of hair and eye, and gloriously naked. His body was well muscled, but smooth as marble, unlike Edward's blond pelt. His hairstyle and his moustache reminded me of old photographs from the 19th century. With his dark hair and eyes, the man should have been olive-skinned like my fantasy image from the first day, but he was as pale as I was, and I had scarcely seen the sun in years. He didn't look sickly, though; if pallor suited everyone as well as it did him, no one would sunbathe ever again.

'You're real!' I said, speaking to him for the first time since those startled cries on the first day. 'I mean, I figured you were real, because you left marks, but you're human.'

'Not exactly, *ma chère*.' The man smiled. His lips were smeared with my blood. His eyeteeth were elongated, curiously sharp, like an animal's fangs. 'Not for several centuries. I am a vampire. Raoul du Plessix at your eternal service.'

It should have terrified me. At least it should have disturbed me a little, knowing that I'd been sharing my bed with a legendary monster.

But it wasn't as though it was a huge surprise. I was a bit unworldly, thanks to living in a sealed world of Edward's making since I was a teenager, but it didn't take a lot of experience to realise sentient, erotically talented mist that turned into a good-looking man wasn't within the realm of the ordinary. I hadn't spent a lot of time speculating about what was going on, though, afraid that, if I examined my phantom lover too closely, he would dissipate back into mist and vanish, and I couldn't bear that. For the first time in nearly ten years, I had something which I could look forward to with joy, not dread.

Knowing Raoul was a vampire didn't bother me as much as it probably would someone who lived a more normal life. But I'd lived for years with a monster in human form, a monster who'd brought me nothing but pain, while my vampire, at least so far, had given me nothing but pleasure.

Even if Raoul ended up draining me of blood, I had a feeling it would hurt less than an ordinary day with Edward. If Raoul killed me, he'd let me slip away on a wave of pleasure, so, until my life drained away, I'd feel joy. And then I'd be free.

'If that is what you wish, Carrie,' Raoul whispered, answering my unspoken thoughts. His voice sounded mournful. 'If your wish is to end your suffering by ending your life, I can ease you into death sweetly. I admit I came to you that first night because I felt your despair and thought you sought death, but your life force is so strong and your passion so sweet it tells me otherwise. Yet I unlocked the door for you these past nights and you never even tried to leave.'

He'd moved up my body as he spoke, so he was lying on top of me, holding his weight on strong arms. His dark eyes bored into me. 'Do you crave death, or do you crave freedom?' he asked in that chocolate-rich accent.

'Freedom,' I answered, not even needing to think. 'But sometimes I'm afraid the only way I'll get it is through death. I was too frightened to leave, even though you've opened the door. I've been trapped for so long.' Then, because I could, because for a few blessed moments I could pretend I really was free, I explored Raoul's broad chest with my hands. He was as cool as the mist to my eager hands, but I already knew he wasn't human, so it didn't bother me.

Warm was overrated. Edward's skin was always feverishly heated.

Edward was the monster, not my vampire.

Raoul moved against my hands like a cat being petted. Still, his face was solemn, and so were his words. 'I can help you, dear one, if you have the courage and the will. You can leave at any time. The world is large. I can help you find somewhere to go.'

'If I just walk out, he'll find me. He'll find me and he'll kill me. Even if he doesn't, I'll be looking over my shoulder for him forever. I tried to run away before,' I said, my voice barely audible. 'I was pregnant. I didn't want to bring Edward's child into the world, but the life inside me hadn't asked to be conceived as the child of rape and abuse. I tried to run to give the baby a chance at a proper life. I wasn't fast enough. He caught me before I could find a safe house. He beat me until I lost the child and nearly lost my life.'

'But after that, at the hospital … does not the law demand such crimes be reported? Or were you afraid to tell the truth about your injuries, about how you came to miscarry?'

'He wouldn't take me to the hospital. He told me a whore who'd made him kill his child didn't deserve medical attention.'

In my pain, I had believed him. Part of me still did. On some level, I wasn't sure I deserved to be free if my first attempt at freedom had cost someone else's life.

Raoul brushed away tears I'd not allowed myself to cry when I miscarried. 'A potential life, not yet a life fully formed – but for the one who carried it close to her heart, precious potential.' I had not spoken my darkest thoughts, and yet he knew them, answered them, comforted me for them. 'You are not to blame. This sorry excuse for a man murdered the child-to-be, as he has tried to murder your spirit. His sin, not yours.'

My few quiet tears turned into full-fledged sobs, the kind I never allowed myself because they'd make Edward feel he had won. I didn't even let myself cry alone any more, lest Edward somehow knew. But with Raoul I could.

A vampire, and yet I felt safer with him than I had with any human I'd ever known, certainly safer than with my mad husband.

Raoul lay down by my side, drew me close. His body was cool against mine, but I could feel the warmth of his spirit through his skin. Still weeping, I whispered, 'Set me free, Raoul. Kill me to do it if you must, or kill him – but I'd rather no one died.'

So many years and I'd never even let myself dream Edward's death – my own sometimes, but not his. In Raoul's arms I could dream a bloody ending to my pain, and to Edward's twisted excuse for a life. I wasn't sure I wanted to make such vengeance a reality, but letting myself imagine it cleansed a long fear that had festered in me.

Raoul brushed my hair out of my eyes. 'I can kill him in a way that looks like an accident. That way, he will never harm anyone again. But you might not be free of him for years, in your heart. Such a death can make you as much a prisoner as he has.' He sounded as if he might know from experience, and I wondered how old he was. 'I could also change you so you are as I am, so he can never harm you again. Nothing mortal could hold you back, and you'd be virtually immortal, but you would trade day for night, and you would crave the taste of blood – usually your lover's, freely given, but sometimes the blood of those who wish to die, or need to die so others are safe – and in other ways you would no longer be human. It is not a choice to take lightly.'

'Change me.' Tears still spilled out of my eyes – I didn't seem to be able to stop, now that I had started – but I writhed my body against his, ran my hands down from his chest to his hard cock which, unlike the rest of him, was warm. 'Being human is overrated, and I've only lived during the nights for so long I won't miss the sun. Set me free, Raoul.' I threw one leg over his hard thigh and guided his cock into my pussy. 'But for now let me forget I'm caged.'

Raoul grabbed my hips and rolled over on to his back, taking me with him.

For a second I froze. 'I don't remember ... I don't know ...' His cock inside me, his body glorious and real, spread under me like a feast, robbed me of words, but I needn't have worried. Raoul, who could read my thoughts, knew what I meant: if I'd ever known what to do when I was on top of a man in bed, I'd long since forgotten. I'd had a boyfriend before Edward, but we didn't date long and we'd rarely had a bed for our awkward experiments, so I came to Edward almost as ignorant as an actual virgin.

'I'll help you, Carrie.'

Raoul set the rhythm at first, using the strength of his lower body to thrust up into me, his hands on my hips to guide me. I leaned forward, letting my hips rise and fall so I rode his cock. At first I followed the rhythm he set, feeling awkward and unsure. Before very long, though, my body realised it knew what it needed and had a pretty good guess what Raoul needed. Kissing his nipples, I worked up and down on his cock, squeezing with muscles that, until a few days ago I'd scarcely known I had. I felt alive and powerful in a way I couldn't remember ever feeling, except maybe as a little girl climbing a forbidden tree or standing, defiant of safety, at the top of the jungle gym.

Pleasure spiralled up from my cunt and my tender swollen clit, spread down from the nipples that rubbed against Raoul's chest. Pleasure exploded from the vicinity of my heart.

I would be free. I would be strong, truly as powerful as I felt in this moment.

I leaned so my throat was in reach of Raoul's mouth and begged, 'Bite me. Do what you need to start the change.'

His fangs closed over my jugular, just like in the movies. Molten silvery pleasure entered where the fangs parted my skin. It snaked through my veins as if it replaced the blood he sipped. It coursed through me until it met the spirals of pleasure rising from where our bodies joined.

I screamed out Raoul's name as I came.

At that moment, Edward's truck growled into the driveway.

I cursed. 'Go!' I yelled, trying to scramble away.

Then I stopped. 'How long would it take to finish making me a vampire?'

Raoul could read my mind all too well. It might become unnerving in time, but at the moment, it was a good thing. Even as I asked the question, he used his fangs, so recently in my throat, to tear open the vein in his wrist. 'Drink,' he said. 'The full change is complex. It will take a night and a day and a night again, and we will need to exchange blood several times to the point of exhaustion – but simply tasting my blood with intention, since I have just taken yours, will start it. You'll be a sort of baby vampire, unable to use all the powers that will be yours, but stronger and faster than your mortal form.'

I was already suckling and licking at the blood pouring from the small wound before he finished speaking. The coppery flavour wasn't as foul as I remembered from all the times my own blood had filled my mouth. Raoul's blood tasted nourishing, like a food that was full of some vitamin my body craved.

He cradled the back of my head as I suckled. 'That's right, Carrie. Take your fill. Every drop will make you stronger.'

I could feel myself changing as I drank. I couldn't tell if my muscles were stronger, or my reflexes sharper, but the dim room seemed bright as a sunny day. I could hear the undertone of Raoul's thoughts – not distinctly, but as a series of misty impressions: pride in me, concern, and an uneasy throbbing of desire, since he'd been unable to come.

I heard Edward's thoughts as well as he banged around downstairs, and they were even uglier than I imagined. He was imagining the scheduler at work, what he'd like to do to her. Imagining hurting other women, or maybe he was remembering doing it. His mind was a red swirl of violence – and he was climbing the stairs.

'He's coming,' I whispered.

'Get behind me,' Raoul mouthed as he slid off the bed.

I didn't, though. Instead, naked and smeared with Raoul's blood and my own, I stood next to my lover as the door burst open.

Edward was silent for a few seconds, as if he couldn't process what he was seeing. Then he howled, literally howled, his anger taking him beyond words. He flew at us, ready, I think to tear us both apart with his bare hands.

I remembered something I'd seen in a kung-fu movie one time. I let him come at me, grabbed his wrist and tossed him aside with a strength and coordination I'd never had before. He hit the ground hard.

'Don't ever touch me again, Edward,' I said. I grinned as I said it, because my gums were tickling and I thought that might mean my fangs were starting to show.

'You have fangs?' Edward looked wildly from me to Raoul. 'You both have fucking fangs! What the hell kind of freak are you fucking, Carrie?'

Raoul bent down over Edward. 'I think you know. I am a creature of blood and mist and the night, the kind that preys on weak bullies like you. And Carrie has joined me. You will never touch her again, never harm her again, never even *think* an unkind word about her or another woman again, or we will find you wherever you hide.'

Edward's eyes widened. He scrambled backwards, propelling himself on his butt, and I laughed, remembering all the times I'd been forced to crab-crawl like that away from him while he hit me and hit me. He managed one last defiant, 'Fine, then. She's a used-up slut anyway. I'll find a good woman this time, one who'll obey me.'

I shuddered, remembering my life with him and my glimpse into his thoughts. I was free of him but, left to his own devices, some other woman would be in his clutches before long. Briefly, I reconsidered my position on killing him, just to keep him from harming anyone else.

Then I had a better idea.

I raised my hand and gestured as Raoul had done to me that first night. 'Sleep, Edward,' I ordered, putting force I didn't know I possessed behind the words. 'Sleep and obey.'

His eyelids fluttered.

'Yes, sleep and obey.' Raoul reinforced my order. 'When you awake, you will not remember me, or remember how Carrie has changed.'

'You won't remember any of this,' I added. 'You may not remember me at all. But you'll feel a compulsion to protect women, to give money to women's shelters, to make sure no woman suffers at a man's hands again.'

'And if you slip up, if you hurt a woman again, we'll know. We're vampires. The night winds and the mists whisper to us,' Raoul intoned. 'And you will regret it.'

Eyes closed, mind clearly lost somewhere, Edward nodded mechanically.

'Sleep until the time you would normally wake up,' I added.

Edward nodded again.

'You will think you had too much to drink and passed out in the spare room.'

Edward curled up obediently and within seconds he was snoring the peculiar raspy way he did when he drank too much – even though he'd come home sober.

Raoul turned to me. 'That was impressive, Carrie. You will make a fine vampire. Not everyone grasps the trick of mind-control so quickly, though I expect we'll have to check on him now and then to make sure he's behaving. But can you turn to mist, I wonder?'

'How do I do it?' But even as I asked him, I knew.

I imagined myself free of everything, including the constraints of having a body. Free as I'd yearned to be.

At first I felt nothing but a strange all-over tickling.

Then I was everywhere and nowhere, and Raoul was everywhere and nowhere with me, mingling with me. It was sexual, powerful, glorious.

Together, we misted into the night, leaving the monster who had been my husband unconscious on the floor of my former prison.

Wolf in the Fold
Monica Belle

Mark Crane checked his look in the mirror. Everything was exactly right. The studied carelessness of his thick dark hair, the two days of stubble, the unaffected rumple of his designer suit. No woman could possibly be indifferent, that he knew. All that remained was to make his selection and the moves that would allow her to surrender to him with her pride intact.

It was getting a little tricky. Abbotsborough wasn't that big and he had been there two years. People were starting to recognise him, and girls he preferred – office types who kept themselves smart and liked to think they were hard to seduce – tended to talk. A few more months and he would have to move on, but for now the challenge was more of a thrill than an obstacle. Tonight he was going in for the kill.

One last glance in the mirror and he moved for the

door where his camel-hair coat hung on the peg, only to hesitate. A copy of the *Abbotsborough Gazette* had been pushed through his letterbox. The headline stood out in bold, black type, a single word – VAMPIRE. He smiled, no more than a derisive twitch to one corner of his mouth, and picked up the paper.

There had been a fifth victim, no more than ten miles away in Alford Wells, a dormitory town no less sleepy than Abbotsborough. The article was the usual stuff, wild speculation without a shred of fact beyond the basic gruesome details. Yet he knew it would be the talk of every bar in town, making the girls frightened, wary, but also vulnerable to the right approach. An amusing notion occurred to him, and instead of putting on his smart camel hair he went to his wardrobe for his ankle-length Australian bush coat and the matching hat.

Wearing it, he looked far from conventional, less attractive, perhaps, to the average woman seeking a well-paid mate, but a little wild, dangerous even, which might net him something rather more interesting. It might also mean he failed, but that wasn't very likely, and, if he did, well, there was always tomorrow night, and the next. After all, while he liked to win, a lot of the pleasure was lost if the victory came too easily.

Outside it was already dark, with the western sky tinged blood-red with a last hint of sunset. The streetlights were on, creating puddles of dull yellow light broken by the shadows of trees and cars. He walked fast, confident in his masculinity and indifferent to others. When he walked, people stepped aside, something he'd been used to for so long he had come to accept it as his due.

By the time he reached the centre of town he had already decided on the preferred setting for his night's work. He was too well known in the bar of the Royal Hotel, where the secretaries of the more upmarket professional firms gathered, and his look wasn't right. Maxamillion's was too flash, the girls too common for his taste, the Bird and Cherry even worse. Aldo's Bar would be best, just so long as there was nobody there who might recognise him.

There wasn't, only a pair of flustered young barmen and the usual mixed crowd of commuters stopping in for a drink on the way home, friends gathered for the evening and staff from the local shops and offices. He ordered vodka, a double measure of Stolichnaya served neat and ice-cold from the fridge. Propping himself against the bar, he sipped his drink and surveyed the room for a possible victim.

Although it was early, there was already plenty of choice. His first thought was a pretty redhead. She was small, the way he liked them, and elegant but with enough curves to spark his interest. Only one thing held him back: her tailored blue uniform, which showed that she worked for the local travel agents. The girl before last had been with the same company, so it was all too likely that her colleagues would be on their guard.

A group of office workers in the window seat looked more promising, especially a sultry brunette with her long stocking-clad legs crossed in such a way that her pin-striped skirt had risen up an impressive length of elegant, toned thigh. It was very easy indeed to image those same perfect legs without clothing in the way, and more, the swell of her hips, her slender waist, her full yet obviously firm chest, her perfect neck; smooth pale skin naked to his caress as she gave in to her feelings, and to his desire.

Mark gave a wry grin for his own thoughts. She was good, but not perfect, too busily engaged in chattering to her friends, while her voice had a high, piping note that would not only be annoying in bed but carried a touch of arrogance. Sometimes that would have been good, as there was always pleasure in seeing a haughty girl melt as she was put through her paces, but not tonight. Tonight he wanted something softer, something more yielding.

One of her companions was a possibility. She sat a little apart from the others, seldom speaking but listening to their conversation with an interest that appeared close to devotion. A fresh face, an unruly mop of brown curls held back with a red ribbon and a cheap suit suggested that she was quite a bit younger than the others, perhaps not all that long out of school. She was appealing too, small but with a figure that held a lot of promise, all the more so for her obvious naivety; a straining blouse, an hourglass waist and good hips that suggested a womanly bottom. Lastly, she was drinking beers and shots, already giggling as her friends urged her to accept another round.

Once again Mark allowed himself a smile. She was just the thing, but there was no rush. He would let her sink a few more drinks, then find an excuse to get talking, perhaps when she went to the Ladies, or came up to the bar for a round. Until then he was content to admire the view, never obvious, but gradually undressing her with his eyes as he speculated on the shape and texture of the flesh now concealed by her jacket and skirt, her blouse and underwear.

He'd ordered a second Stolichnaya and was beginning to wonder just how many beers she could drink without needing a trip to the loo when the door opened to admit a girl who pushed all thoughts of the others from his mind on the instant. She was perfect for what he had in mind: petite, compact, casually dressed and yet smart in a black skirt that clung to her hips and a bright-red roll-necked cashmere jumper tight enough to do more than hint at two pert, upturned breasts beneath. Her hair was a short blonde bob, her eyes large, blue and concealed behind round glasses, all wonderfully yielding, while her sharp, patent-leather heels added a touch of self-conscious display he found irresistible. Best of all, she was carrying a copy of the *Abbotsborough Gazette*, folded, but with the melodramatic headline plainly visible. She was the one, without question.

She was also alone. He moved aside a little and gave her his best friendly grin as she reached the bar. She returned it and glanced up at his face from melting blue eyes, shy and uncertain. A pang of lust hit Mark, so strong that he found himself speaking without time to use one of his extensive range of pre-prepared lines.

'Why don't you let me get that?'

For a moment she looked surprised, before her tiny, full mouth once more curved up into the briefest and faintest of smiles, as if she were scared to show more feeling. Mark took her response as acquiescence.

'What are you having?'

'Cherry brandy, please.'

Her voice was soft, melodic and full of gratitude, as if he'd done her some great favour rather than simply offered to buy her a drink. Maybe, he reflected, that was how she felt. After all, although she was pretty and smartly turned out, she was small and rather mousy, a look not helped by her big owlish glasses. Her choice of drink was also well off the wall, suggesting a lack of social experience that he knew from other encounters might well mean an equal lack of sexual reserve despite her outward shyness. With luck she would give no more than token resistance to his desires, at least until it was too late. He grinned.

'What's your name?'

'Scarlet.'

'As in Johansson?'

He'd meant to follow his remark with a compliment, comparing her to the actress, but seeing the complete lack of comprehension on her face he changed his mind.

'As in O'Hara then?'

Now she understood. 'No. As in the colour.'

'I see. It's a beautiful name. Unusual too.'

'I'm told it suits me.'

He'd been thinking of her as a Lucy, or possibly an Emma, but nodded and smiled. 'It does. I'm just plain Mark.'

'Mark.' She spoke as if savouring his name, and for an instant a small pink tongue flicked out to moisten her lips.

He turned to the barman to sort out the drinks. Her cherry brandy came in a tiny glass, the deep-red liquid releasing a sweet sharp scent that cut through the subtle but intensely feminine musk of whatever she was wearing. He swallowed and found himself resisting an urge to let a hand stray to the front of his trousers in order to make what had suddenly become a badly needed adjustment. Instead he passed her glass to her and raised his own.

'Cheers. Here's to you then.'

Her response was a warm smile, and to raise her own glass in a tentative imitation of his toast to her. Mark took a sip of vodka and spent a moment watching her without speaking. She drank with tiny sips, never allowing her mouth to open more than a fraction, with the result that her lips had quickly begun to take on the rich red colour of the liqueur, as if tainted by a minute release of blood. The image made him feel faint with lust, and he took a full swallow of vodka to clear his head, determined to stay in control. His tone was half joking, half serious as he indicated the paper under her arm. 'You're not afraid of the vampire then?'

She merely shrugged and took another sip of cherry brandy, only to betray her nervousness by spilling a drop, which ran down her chin to create a thin ruby-coloured trail before she hastily wiped it away.

Again Mark felt a surge of lust, repeated as she blushed for her own clumsiness. 'Seriously, though, you ought to be careful.'

He had spoken frankly, implying his ability to protect her without making an overt statement. Again she merely shrugged, but as a huge, heavily bearded man pushed his way to the bar behind her she was forced to move forward, touching him so that he could feel the gentle swell of one breast pressing to his side through their clothes. She had to be aware of the contact, and yet even as the man moved she made no effort to pull away.

For a moment he considered using one of his standard lines, pretending to be in some glamorous job, perhaps a detective on the trail of the vampire. Yet there was no mistaking her body language or the interest in her eyes as she looked up at him, her red-stained lips now just slightly parted to show the crests of small perfectly white front teeth. He wouldn't need to lie, not with this one. She'd fallen, maybe for his looks, maybe for his careful choice of clothes, maybe for something less easily definable, but she'd fallen.

They began to talk, Mark opening one subject after another, first doing his best to draw her out on her own life, and when she responded only with shy and noncommittal answers expanding on his own. She evidently preferred to listen, to his surprise, taking in his words with interest and attention, rarely speaking and never opening her mouth more than a trifle, but with her wide blue eyes gazing up at him with something close to worship but distinctly earthy.

Flattered, he gradually let his guard down, buying a second drink and a third, by which time he knew that it was no longer a question of whether he would be taking her to bed, but only when. Her face was flushed and her cherry-red lips stayed a trifle parted as he spoke to her, betraying her arousal, while their shape and colour worked their own peculiar magic on his need. The colour seemed to grow deeper and more compelling with every sip, until at length he was struggling to hold himself back. He had to have her.

She felt the same, that much was clear. Each time she

moved against him, he could feel the slight bump of one hard nipple. Still she seemed unaware, until with a sudden motion she tugged at the neck of her jumper, as if to allow cool air to her breasts, surely an invitation? Struggling to play it cool, he acknowledged the invitation with only the faintest of smiles, only to give in to his need. She was his, and he could wait no longer.

'It's getting too crowded in here. Would you like to continue this conversation back at my house?'

Her response was a shy nod, urgent for all her seeming inability to express her feelings openly.

'It's just a few minutes' walk. I live alone.'

At last she spoke. 'Take me home with you.'

The honey of her voice alone was enough to make it very clear that she was inviting him not only to take her home, but to bed. He swallowed the last of his drink and led her outside, slipping his arm around her waist as soon as they were on the pavement. She immediately snuggled close, leaving Mark glad he was so much taller than her. His lips had widened to an involuntary grin as he wondered whether she would be quite so easy and so eager had she known what he intended for her.

He kissed her as they reached his house and her response was every bit as urgent as he had hoped. After fumbling the key into the lock, he pushed inside, once more taking her in his arms the instant they were safely alone. He wanted her naked, on her knees with her petite body completely vulnerable, every part of her soft, white flesh exposed to his gaze, and to his hunger. Yet there was still a chance she might escape and he forced himself to confine his attentions to the less provocative parts of her body, stroking her hair and kissing her neck, gently kneading the flesh of her back, until the trembling urgency of her response was simply too much.

Taking hold of either side of her jumper, her pulled it high above her breasts, and buried his face between them, holding one small firm mound in each hand. Her response was a soft mew, like a kitten expecting milk, encouraging him to take advantage of her compliance. Tugging up the cups of her bra, he spilled her naked breasts into his hands, fastening his mouth first to one hard rose-red nipple and then the other. She took hold of his head, holding him to her chest as he attended to her breasts, her breathing now deep and urgent.

Her paper had dropped to the floor, forgotten in their passion, open at the double spread describing the gruesome habits of the vampire. Mark kicked it quickly aside and began to press Scarlet down to the floor, intent on having her right there in the hallway, where he'd be able to nip into the kitchen for what was needed.

To his surprise and annoyance she immediately stiffened, speaking with breathless urgency as she pulled away. 'Not here. Take me upstairs.'

Mark hesitated only a moment, but the time was still

not ripe. Smiling, he took her by the hand and led her upstairs. In his bedroom he made to shrug off his coat, only for Scarlet to shake her head, smiling as she spoke. 'No, keep it on, please, and your hat. You look as if you've been out hunting the vampire.'

It was the first sign she'd given of any real spirit, and Mark grinned in response, more than happy to accommodate her fantasy. Instead of taking his coat off he pushed it open, striking a deliberately dramatic pose.

Scarlet giggled and extended a finger, to draw the tip gently down over his chest, exploring the hard outlines of the muscles beneath his shirt, lower, tracing a line across his taut abdomen, and lower still, to follow the length of the long hard ridge at the front of his trousers. As she touched she gave a low purr, almost a growl, then spoke, her voice soft and rich with promise. 'Why don't you imagine that you are a vampire hunter, and that I'm your prey. You've caught me, but you can't resist me, so you're going to have me ... to do what you like with me ... before you drive a stake right through me.'

As she spoke she had been gently teasing his cock through his trousers, leaving him in no state to refuse had she demanded that he dress up in her underwear and dance for her. With the fantasy she was suggesting there was no difficulty at all, as it wasn't all that far from what he intended. Taking a firm grip on her jumper, he jerked it roughly up and off, pushing with the same motion to send her sprawling on the bed as the garment was pulled off her arms.

She gave a cry of surprise as she fell back, and tried to scramble playfully away. Mark caught her by her skirt, pulling it down over her hips until the waistband would stretch no further. Still she struggled, but he held her firmly in place, enjoying her resistance as he tugged open the button and zip. Her skirt gave way and was pulled quickly down her thighs, leaving her bottom wriggling in black lace panties.

It was a target Mark was unable to resist. He climbed on the bed behind her, snatched at one wrist and twisted her arm behind her back. Again she cried out, her voice showing a little pain, but she made no real effort to stop him, even when he wrenched her panties down at the back and set to work spanking her bottom. She wriggled though, squirming in his grip as her bare cheeks bounced to the firm slaps and begging for mercy she clearly didn't want to receive, and which he had no intention of giving in any case.

Soon her bottom was hot and pink. He began to strip her, still slapping at her bottom as her clothes came off and telling her again and again that she was going to be naked as he pulled off first her hold-up stockings and shoes, her already dishevelled bra and lastly her panties. Only with the final garment did she really begin to struggle, kicking her legs and spitting like a cat as she fought to keep the wispy garment on, although her wild bucking motions as her bottom came fully bare only succeeded in giving him a perfect view of her neatly pursed sex and the tight pink wrinkle between her cheeks.

Even naked and pinned face down on the bed she continued to fight, kicking her thighs in a way that had Mark scrabbling for his fly. She twisted around as he freed his cock, her beautiful eyes wide with emotions that gave her now frantic struggles the lie. Mark returned a meaningful grin, flourishing his cock to let her see exactly what was about to be put inside her. Her response was a hollow groan and she had gone suddenly limp, surrendered to the inevitable.

Holding Scarlet firmly in place, Mark pushed her thighs open with his knees to mount her body. Her flesh felt hot, and firmer than he'd expected, her soft curves hiding a surprising amount of muscle, especially the cheeks of her bottom between which he had nestled his cock. Already fully erect, he needed only to guide himself lower, and in; her sex was moist and receptive to penetration.

Scarlet moaned as she was filled. She was helpless, pinned beneath his weight, her bottom pushed up to receive him, and as he began to thrust into her it was easy to imagine himself as her conqueror. That felt good, taking his pleasure beyond the glorious yet primitive sensation of having his erection sheathed in her body and the resilient flesh of her thighs and heated bottom cheeks against him. It felt good for her too, to judge by her gasping, panting reaction, and he began to wonder what was going through her head. Maybe her need for surrender was so strong that she would give in to what he was about to do to her without a fight?

To judge by the way she was pushing her bottom up it seemed likely, but it was going to happen anyway, his need too strong to be denied. If he hadn't had a chance to butter her, then it wasn't his fault. She should have given in when they were in the hall.

His voice was a grunt as he spoke, simultaneously reaching down to grip his cock. 'This is what I like.'

Scarlet gasped as his cock slid up into the cleft of her bottom, the head pressed between her cheeks and against the tiny hole of her anus. Her voice came as a hiss. 'Bastard!'

'I know. Now just relax.'

She twisted beneath him, but it was too late. He was inside, just a little way, but enough, and as he pushed again she gave what he took for a resigned sob, then spoke. 'At least hold me.'

Her thighs had come wide, surrendering herself. He slipped his hands beneath her, holding her breasts as he pushed himself deeper. She shivered as he began to kiss her face and neck, little mewling noises escaping her throat as she was sodomised. Soon Mark was all the way in, lost in excitement for her helpless surrender as much as in the physical sensation of having his cock sheathed in her bottom and her warm, trembling body in his arms. A few more pushes and he was going to come, his muscles locking in ecstasy as she suddenly twisted her upper body back, her pretty mouth finally coming fully open to the overwhelming sensation of having her anus penetrated, to reveal four small sharp fangs.

Mark was too far gone even to register surprise before she gave a sudden violent convulsion. This time there was no lack of strength in her body. His cock pulled free as he was thrown over on the bed, and even as she mounted him he hadn't fully realised that she was no longer playing a game. His cock was deep in her once more, and he'd begun to come. A vicious, feline hiss escaped her throat as her mouth came wide, exposing her fangs and the red cavity beyond for an instant before she latched on to his neck, sinking her teeth deep and hard.

He screamed, his body still tight in orgasm even as her fangs met in his neck, tearing flesh and bursting veins. Terror welled up in his mind, and panic. He began to jerk in her grip, just as she had in his only moments before, but she was impossibly strong, holding him helpless as she worried at his neck, fangs thrust down to the bone as a cat kills a rat. A last plea broke from his lips as his vision began to blur, but there was no mercy, his senses slipping away and his body going slowly limp as Scarlet began to feed.

Rent
Angela Caperton

In the doorway, Anise bounced the key in her hand while the tall young man explored the best room available to rent. He poked at the bed and looked around the little chamber.

'Bathroom's down the hall. Nora serves breakfast at seven, dinner at six. No guests after nine.'

'How much?' The young man's name was Isaac. He appeared to be no more than 22 years old, with nice skin and a healthy pulse.

'Ten a week,' Anise said with a lazy drawl. She pulled at the lace of her cuff absently as she appraised him.

'Ten. How about eight?'

Anise held her smile. 'Ten. You're in the Market district, young man, and, along with the room, two meals are guaranteed.'

'I can't do ten.'

'Try the east side.' She stepped out of the doorway, her message clear. He could take it or leave it.

Handsome young Isaac curled the brim of his hat and stepped past her. She sensed his disappointment. The bare bulb in the hallway flickered as she reached out to stop him, her touch insistent, needy, but controlled. His warmth and masculine scent intoxicated her. He stiffened in her grip. She thought of a bird in a cat's jaws as her long ashen fingers brushed his arm. He shifted his hat as if it were a shield. She leaned close, her breath just brushing his ear. 'Are you good with your hands?'

His trousers tented, the stiff erection a sweet reminder of what she had been, what she was and would always be. She didn't need to beguile him with anything more than mortal desire.

'Yes, ma'am,' he said. 'I am. I can fix almost anything. Make it hum – like new.'

'Oh, I have no doubt of that.' Anise pulled him back into the room and to the narrow bed. 'Take your clothes off,' she ordered him.

'Listen,' he started, but she kissed him, taking away his choices along with his breath, unfastening his shirt, popping the buttons on his pants so they clattered around the room. In a moment, Isaac lay back on the bed stark naked, his long cut cock rising up like the phallus of an ivory demigod.

I'll keep this one awhile, Anise thought, as she settled on him, savouring the slow slide of his heat into the chill space between her legs. Someday perhaps she would understand why some men stirred new fire, while others only filled space. Her blood flowed again, warmed, a return of pure sugar in the cane, new life, new joy. She rose and settled again, pulling him with her hands and her will, matching his rhythm to hers, using him but pleasing him, her living toy.

He thrashed and she held him with the most natural of glamour, the perfect, practised grip of her cunt, hot now with his life. She rode, with abandon, then bent down and bit his throat, drinking the gush even as she made him come, rolling him in her pussy, milking him, coming herself, in reds and colours brighter than the sun. This was life.

This was simple eternity.

Anise watched him sleep, tenderness almost overwhelming her. The best times gave her vivid memories of a time long gone. Today, Isaac had given her life again. For now, that was enough. She woke him with a kiss, rising to straighten her skirt and button her blouse.

He blinked and looked up at her. 'Anything,' he pledged. 'I will give you anything.'

She kissed his lips, then licked the trickle on his neck. He laughed, a breathy, desperate sound.

'Just the rent,' Anise whispered. 'Once a month.'

* * *

Isaac would do for now, but she needed one more tenant. One more room remained unfilled.

She'd lived in the new world, in America, for almost eighty years, had turned her back on the byzantine intrigues of the old lords in Europe and on the eastern coast of America, rejecting them and their laws. She came to San Francisco with a hope for easy existence, and to some extent she had found it. Her first year there, the city had been almost destroyed by an earthquake, but she had found purpose helping, in her own way, to rebuild the city from its ruins.

In the fifth year after the great quake, she had bought the boarding house and, in the twenty years since, she'd screened her tenants carefully. All of them provided sustenance and, through time, she'd learned to rotate her stock. Isaac would replace the actor she had watched grow from bit player to star. Had Anise's influence been a part of his rise to fame? She liked to think so, but that had never been her purpose. His success did not especially please her – she hated to see him go – but she found herself proud of him.

Now, in 1931, with the new disaster of financial ruin still shaking the land, she found her own life had become easier. The passage of seekers west across the dusty continent became more insistent and more desperate. She had grown almost complacent in satiation.

She smelled the prospective tenant approaching, outside on the walkway. She instantly sensed an aura of threat about him and she analysed her feelings, what she garnered from his scent and from the aura of emotion that all mortals projected. This one reeked of contradictions, a rich danger in his blood, the sharp want that pulsed in the space between his righteous quest and her anticipated, brazen temptation. He might be the one. He'd feed her, yes, but would he sustain her soul, give her reason to look beyond each sunrise to seek the possibility in the shadows?

The knock was direct, almost arrogant. Her pussy ticked with each hard rap, one, two, three. She answered the door with a smile, the misty rain beyond the threshold more than welcome. He smiled back almost apologetically when he crossed the threshold, shaking the drops of rain from his hat.

'Ma'am,' he said, confident. No false flattery in trying to pretend she was less than her apparent age. Anise refused to mask the natural face of her existence. She accepted 'ma'am' as she might a bunch of posies. 'Ma'am' held a special power, a delicious richness. Young men learned from older women.

'You're looking for a room?' she asked, although Anise knew the last thing on his mind was a bed and meals. She savoured his scent and the quickened beat of his heart pounded a rhythm for the dance that was about to begin. She could read his emotions but not his thoughts, though his intentions were as clear as the vein in a drying leaf.

He didn't answer, but looked at her for several moments, the intensity of his gaze as hot as sunlight. 'Sure,' he finally said.

Something's wrong. Cutting the sweet haze of lust and anticipation, a warning sounded like a herald's horn in her mind.

Pushing aside the feeling, Anise strode by him, up the stairs. 'Rent's ten a week, breakfast at seven, dinner at six.' She smiled, her back to the man, living the role she guessed that he had already seen through. She blushed red with the memory of bloodflow as she tasted his uncertainty, the hot caution that warred within him.

Her own misgivings spelled out their message through the gates of her expanded senses. *He carried cross and stake; she smelled silver chains in his bag.* But it was his wavering certainty that topped her confection.

He had come here to kill her, but would he first fuck her? Her spirit rose at the challenge. Could she seduce him without the shimmer of glamour, the unnatural allure of her true self? She knew she should just turn and snap his neck, kill him before he tried to kill her. A hundred years ago, he wouldn't have made it past the foyer, but in this place, with Isaac and Martin docile in their rooms, this one offered more than food. He offered excitement, and, more than anything, Anise hungered for novelty.

Eternity lacked the burn of finality. Here was a chance to taste risk again. Death glistened at the tip of his stake, a cold counterpart to the pearl of desire that would tip his cock. She smelled his arousal, but didn't know if he was stimulated by sex or the promise of violence. Uncertainty annoyed her. She wanted to taste the salt, wanted his jumpy prick to tap against her fangs. So easy to close her jaws and fill her mouth with precious, thick nectars, white and red.

She maintained the charade, led him up the broad wooden stairs to the little room on the third floor. Beyond the heavy door, bed and dresser dominated the space, a cheap little painting hung lifelessly beside the stingy closet.

She had the sense of being in a play where both actors had secret lines, memorised but unspoken because they would break the spell of normality and leave the charade in ruins.

'Bathroom's downstairs on two, end of the hall.' Anise smiled as he stepped into the centre of the little chamber.

He pretended to be interested, pulled the curtains aside and stared out through small glass panes, across a vista of spotty tiles on the roof of the house next door. 'Eight,' he offered.

'Ten. Catch the cable east if you want something cheap.'

'Eight.' He closed the distance between them as smoothly as one of her kindred might, but with the rich, live cream of flesh and pulse. His arm curled around her waist, pulled her hips against his, hard, demanding and controlled. His cock wasn't jumping, but it was firm, a disciplined erection, and Anise's sex churned. 'Eight and I'll give you something you can't resist.'

Anise laughed. 'You think I'm lonely, that I'm easy? Ten.'

His smile shivered her spine. 'I think you're bored, and I know what you are. Eight.'

Her body melded against his, line for line, muscle to muscle. His breath warmed the chill flesh of her neck. His hands kneaded muscle and bone that yielded under the warmth of his touch. She wanted his cock inside her, but didn't want to bend him to it. No, no, he was right. He knew her. He knew what she wanted, sex born of real desire, not from glamour.

'And for eight, what will you do for me?' Anise teased, her fangs brushing against the thick pulse at his neck, her mouth watering like her cunt.

He gripped her arms hard enough to bruise, were she capable of bruising. He crushed her to him, but denied his neck to her dripping fangs. His forehead pressed to hers, shielding his gaze from hers by proximity, their closeness a mirage of shadow and colour. His lips brushed her mouth, a violent tease that crushed her unbeating heart with want. 'For eight, I won't kill you.'

'Who are you,' she asked, 'to come into my house and threaten me?'

'A rent collector,' he said, and he cupped her bottom through her dress and slip, his grip implacable and insistent.

Intrigued, she asked, 'For what landlord?'

'You know him. Back east. I saw your portrait on his wall.' Silver jingled as he withdrew a length of thin chain from his trouser pocket.

A part of her wanted the cleansing fire against her skin, wanted him to bind her in pain, shackle her to the narrow bed and fuck her with the stake of his cock, but she caught his wrist with the least of her strength and stayed the moment. His surprise delighted her.

'Brave man to come here. Or maybe just stupid.' She considered turning him around, against his will, bending him over and claiming him with her hand, then ravishing his will, leaving him no choice but to fuck her until he was dry.

'If you kill me, another will come,' he said. 'The lords of the east are looking for new fields. The fortunes of a thousand years have been wiped out and they need reseeding.'

She had heard something about this from one of the few sisters she knew, a woman who worked in movies down in Hollywood. Three or four of the most powerful vampires in New York and Boston sought to recover what they had lost by exploring the possibilities out here on the golden coast.

'Do they mean to make new children?' she asked him. As far as she knew, it had been over a hundred years since a mortal had been turned. Eternal life was the rarest of gifts and no one granted it lightly. 'Is that what they promised you?'

'You want me to tell you my price?' He smiled, but she felt his unease in the pulse within the strong arm she held effortlessly.

'No, I really don't care. You are welcome here if you want to stay. Do what you must.'

She eased her grip on his wrist, kissing his forehead, so that he raised his eyes and looked into hers. She saw a little fear, but far more intriguing options shimmered in the pools of soft brown. She pushed past him, a lithe press against him as she moved. 'Eight, then.'

He reached into his pocket and pulled out crisp dollar bills. 'First week's payment, ma'am.'

'Anise. You may call me Anise. And what is your name?'

'Charles Kurtzwald. Is Anise your real name?'

'It is today.' She slid past him and down the hall, not looking back, though she wanted to with a desire as compelling as sunset.

* * *

For two weeks, Anise watched Charles come and go, listened to him walk around the small room on the top floor, grinned when the thin, rhythmic squeak of the bed frame betrayed his masturbation. She touched herself, listening, wondering just what kind of cock he had – long, thin, thick, cut or uncut? She had a vague sense from their first encounter, but clothing could be deceiving. She'd found joy in all varieties, and longed to taste his. She could easily enter his room and take her fill, but that wasn't what she wanted and, she suspected, it would ruin any chance of making him what she had come to believe he might be.

They'd talked late in the night, after Nora had left and the other tenants had taken to their beds. Politics, literature, commerce, art, music. No subject escaped their touch and Anise grew to value the precious night hours they spent together. He made no attempt to harm her, his mission simultaneously a bond and a barrier. She thought he had grown to value her company just as much as she cherished his. What they didn't talk about was why he was there.

Nor did they fuck. She calmed the urgency of her own need, taking blood from her other tenants, but tamping down her desire for sex, savouring the anticipation for what it would be like when she and Charles came together.

Then he went away a few days, travelling to some purpose he did not share, though she guessed it had something to do with his assignment ... his duty to subjugate or slay her. When he returned, he seemed withdrawn, quiet when she tried to talk to him. He paid his rent in cash and his eyes betrayed his torment.

Damn them! she thought.

She resented that some pompous goat from the old country had decided that her house was his for the taking. She had come to the new world and then on to California to escape the leaden tyranny of the old lords. When she was young, she had signed some sort of agreement of fealty, to the surrender of gold and property on demand of the elders, the ones who had made her what she was. She wondered if somewhere there were books of vampiric law that governed the lien against her life in death. Did she owe them eternally or only for decades or for centuries?

The laws of silver and sacred things were inviolate, but surely the lords created other laws, as men make theirs, for convenience and ease, for the oppression of those they deemed inferior? The thought made her furious.

All her dealings with the old lords had left her determined to escape them and so she had come out here, to a land where few of her kind had ever walked the midnight ways. The act had been an affirmation and a defiance, and she would not roll over at their whim. Not this time. She wasn't starry-eyed or unsure of herself any more. She had stayed safe and hidden, autonomous and, if not content, then at least at peace in most seasons.

Angry at her own concern, she rose from her bed,

looking up at the ceiling. Charles was not up there; he was gone again on night-time business.

Just what was he up to these days?

The next night he came through the door close to midnight. She sat in the parlour, her skin flush with Martin the stevedore's recent payment, the taste of blood still salty in her throat. Charles removed his coat, shaking off the damp, and Anise knew that tonight was the night. She moved to his side before the next beat of his heart.

'Charles,' she whispered, wickedly tickled by his jump.

'Anise, good evening,' he managed with a cool tone, though the rapid pulse that beat in his throat made her mouth water.

'How long do we have, Charles?'

He knew her meaning: how long before those old bastards called him due or sent another to finish what he hadn't?

'Not long. Maybe another week or two.' He reached out and stroked her long grey-streaked hair, the caress tender.

She nodded and took his hand, pulling him down the hall to the stairs that led to the basement and her rooms.

At the top of the stairs he stopped, pulling back to force her to look at him. His gaze opened to her even as his expression remained controlled. 'What's down there?'

'I am. Will you join me?'

He stood stock still, his gaze turning hard, as if her

invitation had broken a precious artefact on a shelf. 'I won't pay my rent this way.'

Anise's smile turned to smoke. 'I never thought you would. Come.'

She squeezed his hand and led him down the stairs.

Candles turned spots of the interior to gold, but most of the space was dark, though Anise led Charles easily to her bed. Unhesitating, she took his mouth with hers, a devouring kiss he met with equal zeal. He tasted green as a sea of grass, vast, mysterious and full of life. His warmth intoxicated her and his hunger excited her in ways she'd thought nothing more than memory. She pulled his shirt loose from the waist of his pants, contemptuous of the buttons as she tore it apart, exposing his chest, the thunder of his heart deafening. She relished the sensations of his muscles and stroked the thin line of hair that tickled down the centre of his belly to disappear beneath the waistband that had become an intolerable barrier.

He gripped her arms, hindering her exploration and sparking a feral violence that nearly crippled her control. She allowed him to use his strength to hold her, to keep her from what she wanted, and, while Anise knew she could break his arms like sticks, his resistance to her power gratified her in a way she'd not known for more than a century. She was so accustomed to wielding her will like a knife, emasculating her lovers, moulding them into what she wanted – sustenance and sex. She'd never touched Charles in that way, and she never would. He wanted to undo her and she found she too wanted that, needed that, needed the thrill of his masculinity, the acid danger of his dominance, even if he chose to kill her. She rubbed against him, her pussy wet and ready, her fangs stinging against the excitement of his heated skin so close, so tender.

The jagged ripping of her blouse spiked her lust, a silent sigh burning her throat, begging for release. She needed him inside her, deep, hard, his cock striking the core that still lived, still pulsed and longed to be bruised, the joyous slide of his flesh into hers, the ultimate claiming that she had for so many years cheated.

She had taken lovers by the dozen, but none of them had taken her.

She wouldn't touch his will, vowed to open to him, whole and as close to alive as she could ever be. She tossed the dice and turned herself over to trust and gave it what she no longer possessed, the fresh breath of life. Men and sex had been payment for a roof and food, but this man offered far more than that. She relaxed in his arms, let his mouth claim her breasts and savoured his bite, blunt but powerful, on her nipples, the lapping of his tongue fanning the growing heat inside her. Her blood thinned, her vision dimmed, a glorious haze of pleasure falling over her like a blanket.

Their remaining clothes melted in tugs and tears and,

when she fell on her bed, him upon her, they tangled like silk strands blown in a summer gale. She locked her legs around his hips, rubbed the warming wetness of her pussy against the hard length of his cock and her body sang with the tremble and jump of that precious flesh. He stroked and plied, kissed her to panting, and, when she thought she could not take another moment, he sat up, pulling her hips against his, his pearl-crowned cock poised at the gate.

'This doesn't change anything,' he said, pressing just the slick head between her ready lips.

Anise arched against him, rubbing her wetness along his length, feeling the flow of blood there surge again. 'No, but perhaps ...'

He growled, an animal sound that made her want to laugh with delight, but, before the bubble could rise from her belly, he gripped her hips and flipped her over, prone, vulnerable. She imagined a stake in his hand, flashing and cruel, driven between her shoulder blades, and she surrendered to him.

In the moment that she prepared to fall into the void, she smelled it like the faded scent of a rose pressed in the pages of a book – he could not kill her. She hung on the moment, naked and helpless beneath him and he drove into her, his rigid cock invaded, plundered, took her, pushing deep into her core so that the pain she had imagined, the pointed wood parting her flesh, melted to golden pleasure, his thrust true and sure. He wrapped her long hair in his hand, pulled her head back as he fucked her – *fucked her*, each thrust a possession, a lesson hard learned. Her flesh clenched around him as she pushed back, wanting him deeper, splitting her reason from her senses, epically blinding her to all possibilities other than the raging pleasure he bestowed. She bucked back and ground against his hips, her arms trembling with the building orgasm. He leaned over her, clamping his teeth into her shoulder, a savage claiming that left her mindless, the closest she had been to life in so very long a time. He pressed her into the bed, his rhythm driving her close to the edge of oblivion.

She gave herself over to him then, surrendering the last of her resistance, as pliant as though she were truly mortal, bound by the savagery of his desire, the power of his hands, one still tangled in her hair, the other finding her clit and pressing. He thrust entirely into her, coming, his teeth in her shoulder in a divine reversal of roles.

Anise knew her body in death even as she had known it in life. She knew the path to orgasm well and travelled it effortlessly, whether by her own hand, by the tongue of a practised servant or by the cock of one of her tenants, but what rolled over her now seared white hot, an unknown truth so long a mystery to her. Sensations richer than any she had ever known, a taste of honey on her tongue, spasms of pleasure so strong they almost hurt, every inch of her flesh aroused and expending in light and heat.

She screamed and clenched around his cock, bucking under him, her strength uncontrolled now so that he bounced atop her for a moment, holding tight with ecstatic determination. She loved that he would not let her go, that they thrashed together, one flesh, one soul, half living and half dead, but whole.

They lay side by side, his arms around her. The joy of tenderness swam against her for ages. There were a thousand questions she wanted to ask, but she could not bring herself to steal even a second from her happiness.

'They promised me anything I want,' he said. 'A fortune, this house, worldly power of every sort.'

She ached with disappointment that he might be bought so cheaply.

'But that's not why I came.'

His words teased the ashes of her regret. 'Why then?' she asked.

'I came because of the stories they told me about you, because every time I heard your name, the stories they told ... the portrait of you I saw in one of their halls ... I had to see you. I had to know.'

She propped herself up on one arm, regarding the rise of his chest, the sweetness of his breathing. 'To know what?'

'To know if what I felt was only delusion. To know if what I felt was love.'

She didn't need to ask more. His heart beat, and within her ribs an echo matched the pulse.

'So what now?' she asked. 'What do we do?'

'Whatever we need to,' he said, rising to look into her eyes. 'The world is big. We don't have to stay here.'

He kissed her and she let him pull her tight against his broad warm chest. Would she be able to give him her gift? So many found it a curse. Life radiated from him. Could she turn him cold? She would, if he wished it. She would thumb her nose again at those lords if Charles wished it. There was no greater transgression than turning a mortal without their permission, but she didn't care.

Forever or for only a season, she knew she and Charles would be one, their lease on life a bond beyond measure.

And when the rent came due, they would find a way to pay it together.

A Strigoi in Rome
Morwenna Drake

Caecilia shed her robe and lowered herself into the scented waters. The rose perfume tantalised her senses as the warmth enveloped her, the water caressing and lifting her breasts up as she sank down further.

'The jasmine oil, I think,' she said. She leaned back and closed her eyes, feeling the tension of the day soak out of her muscles. She tried not to think about the banquet that night, which would be trying. It had been easy enough when her father had married her to Antonius; he had been the obvious suitor. But now, after Antonius' death, her father seemed to be taking his time finding her a new husband. She was indifferent to whom he chose – one man was as dull as another – but she did so hate being on display at these dinners like a horse in the marketplace.

Her slave, Klymene, knelt behind her and began

brushing out Caecilia's hair before fetching the jasmine oil as ordered. She massaged oil into one of Caecilia's arms then fetched an ivory strigil and with a sure stroke scraped the oil from Caecilia's skin and rinsed it with clean water. Klymene repeated the task on Caecilia's other arm and her back, until Caecilia felt her skin was glowing.

'That is a nasty mark you have on your neck, mistress,' Klymene observed as she poured more oil on to her hands.

'I noticed that this morning,' said Caecilia sleepily. 'I can't think where it came from. Maybe you were careless with one of my hairpins.'

'I would not be so careless,' Klymene replied defensively.

Caecilia held back a sigh. Her father often complained she allowed Klymene too free a tongue, and sometimes Caecilia wondered if he was right.

'Perhaps not, but I can think of no other explanation.'

'They look like bite marks, mistress.'

Caecilia's eyes snapped open and her shoulders tensed, a memory hovering on the edge of recollection. It was dark, but with the smell of lilies, so she must have been by the fountain in her father's garden. Her senses were dulled by wine but she could recall someone sitting beside her on the stone bench, a man with a shadowy face. He kissed her, tasting of wine and honey, smelling of spices. She closed her eyes as his lips traced across her skin and down her jaw. Caecilia frowned as she tried to remember what had happened next. The vague recollection of pain skittered over her mind, but the next thing she remembered was sitting peacefully in her room, looking out of the window.

'Bite marks? On my neck? I am sure I would remember something like that.' The frown on Klymene's face both angered and frightened Caecilia. 'What do you know, Klymene? Tell me.'

'I know nothing, mistress. Only a story that my people would tell children to keep them good.'

The water suddenly seemed chilled as it lapped around Caecilia. She forced her voice to be light-hearted. 'Tell me, Klymene. I'd like to hear. There will be such dull talk at Father's table tonight. Give me a story to keep me entertained while I smile like a statue at them all.'

Klymene regarded her for a moment then shrugged and poured out more oil. Caecilia leaned back in the bath, closing her eyes again, trying to regain the peace of a few moments ago.

Klymene massaged Caecilia's shoulders as she spoke. 'I was thinking of the Empusa, mistress. My mother told me the tale, as we sat around the fire in the depths of winter. It would make my little brother, Akakios, cry but my mother would tell it just the same. The great goddess Hecate, who watches over witches and travellers, had a spirit servant named Mormo. He was besotted with her, but it was a dark, jealous love.'

Klymene's skilled hands drew the tension from

Caecilia's shoulders as Caecilia's mind drifted, imagining a powerful goddess atop a throne of flowers, skulls and candles. Klymene's voice was soothing, even when she spoke of dark things.

'One night, Mormo tricked the goddess with drugged wine and lay with her. When she awoke, Hecate was furious yet impressed by Mormo's cunning. When the union produced a child, she named it Empusa and fed her on the blood of snakes.'

Klymene's hands moved from Caecilia's shoulders, over her breastbone. Caecilia shifted slightly, raising herself up a little.

'Empusa was an ugly, twisted thing, the product of trickery. Yet she was also born of love, even if that love was as twisted as her limbs, so she had an element of beauty within her. When she was hungry, she drew forth this beauty and assumed the guise of a beautiful woman.'

Klymene's fingers found Caecilia's nipples and massaged oil around them. They hardened under her fingers and little sparks of heat travelled down Caecilia's belly. Caecilia's fingers traced the same path, below her navel to toy with her lower curls.

'Empusa would wait at crossroads and, when a weary lost traveller passed her way, she would offer them succour. She would lead them to a nearby cave, one she had transformed into a room lavish enough to rival any palace. She would ply the traveller with wine, spiced figs

118

and tender chunks of lamb. When they were sated by wine and food, she would awaken other desires.'

Caecilia's fingers slipped from her curls into her soft intimate flesh. The hidden skin was hot, slippery with water and arousal. Klymene's hands continued massaging Caecilia's breasts, kneading them and tweaking her nipples. Caecilia arched her back as she slipped her own fingers inside, searching for that sweetest of spots.

'Empusa's fingers would weave a cunning spell about the traveller's flesh. When their skin was hot with lust, she would lead them to a fur-lined bed, lay them down and undress them. Their manhood would spring tall and proud, and she would take it inside her, riding them until they screamed her name.'

Caecilia's fingers found their prize and she drew circles inside herself, feeling heat and pleasure building in her body as Klymene's words drifted around her. 'This she would do for hours, until the sun was almost up and the traveller was on the point of exhaustion.'

Caecilia arched her back as an orgasm swept through her, the water splashing over the sides of the bath on to the tiled floor.

As the spasms died away, Klymene softly whispered the conclusion to her tale.

'Then, as the traveller lay sleeping, Empusa would bite down on their skin, draining their blood until a white withered corpse was all that remained. Then the lavish palace would return to a dank cave, the sun would rise and Empusa would vanish, until she became hungry again.'

A shudder ran through Caecilia, but she chased it away with a laugh and stood up. 'No wonder your little brother cried. That is quite a story, Klymene.'

'Does my mistress feel less tense now?' Klymene asked with a satisfied smile, as Caecilia stepped out of the bath.

'Indeed. You are a wonder with that oil, Klymene. Now, dry me and dress me. And find a gold torque to hide these – whatever they are – on my neck.'

Caecilia was dressed and in the culina, overseeing preparations, when her father emerged from his own rooms wearing a fine white toga lined with deep blue. He cast an appraising glance over her outfit – an elegant tunic of cream linen which fell almost to the floor, but was slit up one side to her hip. Caecilia knew how her father liked her to mix just the right amount of respectability with flesh, especially when the purpose of the banquet was to find her a new husband.

Priscus nodded approvingly before asking, a little anxiously, 'Is the gustatio nearly ready, Caecilia? Our guests will be here within the hour.'

Caecilia planted a kiss on his cheek and gave a reassuring smile. 'Has Tychon ever failed us before? The gustatio is nearly done, and will be on the table waiting for our guests just as they drain their goblets.'

Priscus gave a weary, but genuine smile. 'I have no faith in slaves, but I know you would never fail me, dear daughter. Shall we?' He took her arm and led her into peristylum, the open courtyard and garden, where they awaited the arrival of their guests.

The dinner was as tiresome as Caecilia had anticipated. Her father was a different man when among senators and businessmen. Priscus had made his fortune trading first in wool, then in cloth, and finally adding dyes to his list of exports. Those around the table were a mixture of old trading friends who, like Priscus, had grown in power, and new acquaintances who were rising fast. Caecilia knew their names but cared little for much beyond that. She would take more of an interest when she knew to which of them her father intended to marry her. For now, her duty was to look as appealing as possible.

The gustatio had indeed been ready on the table when they entered the dining room and slaves brought in more dishes once all the guests were seated. As a slave ladled cooked clams into her bowl, Caecilia's eyes drifted to the only interesting person at the table, a man called Silvanus. She had met him for the first time at the private dinner her father had held a week ago. He was the stranger from the garden, the one whose kiss had been so ... forgettable. As he discussed the perils of sea trade with a fish merchant next to him, Caecilia took the opportunity to look him over more closely.

His skin was coloured, but not tanned, and somehow still seemed pale. His eyes were a deep green, as if part of the forest he was named for had been captured within them. He was lean but lithe, like a cat. His arms were muscled, but from exercise rather than labour. His hair brushed his ears, sleek and chestnut.

As if feeling her eyes upon him, Silvanus looked up and Caecilia blushed. She turned, starting up a conversation with one of Priscus' captains, yet she could still feel Silvanus' eyes upon her. It felt as if a candle flame was passing close to her skin, warming the flesh as it passed.

Throughout the second and third courses, Caecilia snatched glances at Silvanus, but his gaze was never on her and she felt its loss like the sun passing behind a cloud. When the slaves brought in dishes of almond cakes, pomegranates and stewed pears, Caecilia's glance alerted her to the fact that Silvanus was missing. Curiosity made her rise and excuse herself.

The atrium was empty, with all the guests in the dining room and the slaves in the kitchen. Caecilia stood in the shadows, wondering, before a soft gasp drew her towards the peristylum. The sun had set and the moon risen into a clear sky. Candles and oil lamps lit the house, but the slaves were too busy to bring light to this quiet corner.

Caecilia made her way silently through the plants, her eyes scanning the darkness. As she neared the pool, she saw two figures standing beside it. Even in the gloom,

Silvanus' striking figure was recognisable. In his arms, almost limp, was a slave girl, her head tilted back as Silvanus kissed her neck hungrily. It was the girl's gasp that had drawn Caecilia and jealousy suddenly burned within her chest.

She stepped out of the shadows, standing tall and straight and speaking in a clear voice. 'Silvanus, isn't it?'

The slave girl bolted upright, all limpness gone. She adjusted her grease-smeared tunic and hurried away, her head bowed away from her mistress' eyes. Silvanus turned and sat down on the bench in one graceful movement.

'Ah, the widow. Or is it the daughter? Tell me, which do you see yourself as tonight?' With a grin, he patted the empty space next to him.

Caecilia hesitated only a moment before she took it. 'Tonight, I believe I am the meat,' she replied dryly.

Silvanus raised an eyebrow. 'Then you are a dish fit only for the tongue of Scipio.'

'Scipio?' Caecilia frowned as she tried to recall the guests' faces. She brought to mind a relatively young man, with thick arms and a serious face which softened when he smiled. 'He's just been made a quaestor, if we are thinking of the same man.'

'In my experience, a man who oversees the money of the realm oversees the realm itself. The word is that he is your father's first choice for a second son-in-law. Do you approve?' He reached down behind the bench towards a goblet of wine. As he leaned forward, closer to Caecilia, the warm smell of spices surrounded her and made her head spin.

'Why should my opinion count? I will marry whomsoever my father chooses for me. What else are daughters for?'

Silvanus drained the goblet. 'I have no daughters so cannot say. But I do know what women are for. Tell me, were you happy in your last marriage?' His stare was suddenly intense, as if he was reading the answer in her mind.

'I believe so,' Caecilia said cautiously. 'I have no other marriage with which to compare it. My husband was an old man and living with him, caring for him, was much like living with my father.'

'But not in exactly the same way, I hope?' Silvanus asked, laughter on his lips.

'I am sorry?'

'What I mean, little bird, is that there are some services a woman renders to her husband, which a daughter would never give to her father.'

Caecilia stiffened. It did not seem right to discuss such things with a trader who had been in Rome less than a month, yet the words seem to come before she could stop them. 'Indeed. I performed those services too.'

'And?' When she merely looked at him askance, he prompted, 'In my experience, those services are among the more enjoyable that a wife must perform. Do you not agree?'

Like a magician, from the shadows he produced a jug of sweet wine. He filled the goblet and offered it to her. She drained it in three mouthfuls. The alcohol set a fire in her belly to match the one that was smouldering lower down in the presence of this enigmatic stranger.

'I enjoyed them well enough,' she replied carelessly, 'much like sewing or baking. And, like those activities, I find that women are far superior to men.'

'Really? You think a man less skilled in that area?' His voice was serious, but his eyes held a playful gleam.

Caecilia straightened, trying to look commanding despite the fever playing across her skin. 'I think a man is skilled when it comes to his own interests, and a woman with hers.'

'Is that so?' he asked wryly.

He reached out, his fingers sliding beneath her tunic to caress the bare skin of her leg. Caecilia knew she should rise and run to her father, declaring Silvanus' infamy, yet she also knew Silvanus was playing a game, and that she would lose if she fled. So instead, she parted her legs and leaned back, a challenging look in her eye, even as her heart hammered at such boldness.

Silvanus stroked lazily across her thigh, caressing the top of her curls. He moved closer, his leg pressing against her. Glancing down, Caecilia saw an unmistakable bulge in his tunic that stirred excitement within her.

His fingers descended lower, parting her flesh until they found her bud. He rubbed it gently but firmly, sending spikes of desire shooting through her. Caecilia was breathing hard as his thumb took over and his fingers slid lower, slipping inside her. A gasp rose to her lips but he trapped it there with a deep kiss. As his fingers found her sweet spot, Caecilia shuddered and would have cried out but for his lips on hers. She came with a violent shudder, which left her body trembling as he stood up and adjusted his toga.

'Perhaps you will revise your opinion now, my lady? And in doing so, perhaps I have done our friend Scipio a service.' He gave her a slight bow and flashed a wicked smile. In the gloom, it seemed that two of his teeth had elongated, as if he was turning into a beast, but the impression was fleeting as he turned and left her alone.

* * *

'You will be careful today, mistress?' Klymene said as she fussed over Caecilia's hair.

Caecilia put down the bronze mirror and turned with puzzlement to her slave. 'Careful? Why should a slave need to warn me about visiting a trader's house? I have visited many with my father. You cluck like an old hen, Klymene.'

'Many traders, yes. But not like Silvanus, mistress. His reputation is spoken only in whispers.'

'Honestly, Klymene. A few days ago it was the Empusa, now it is sordid gossip about a respectable trader.'

'They may be one and the same thing, mistress,' she said in a low voice that startled Caecilia. 'After the night of the banquet, young Xanthe had marks on her neck, just like yours, mistress. And Tychon said one of the boys had seen her go into the garden with Silvanus.'

Caecilia thought of the slave girl she had found limp in Silvanus' arms, and unease stole through her.

'They say that Silvanus' villa is a place where pain and pleasure cannot be distinguished. Men go in filled with lust and come out drunk on blood.'

'That is ridiculous,' Caecilia snapped irritably. 'Silvanus is no more corrupt than any other man in Rome. And if he did bite that wretched girl, it was probably in a moment of passion. Now cease twittering and finish dressing me.'

Klymene bit her lip but said nothing further.

When Caecilia was dressed, she went to the atrium and her cloak was brought to her by Xanthe. Before the slave turned away, Caecilia caught her by the arm and pushed back the lank hair to see two perfect puncture marks, similar to the ones hidden beneath Caecilia's necklace.

She dismissed the girl, and her irritation was replaced by a cold dread. She made her way out to the covered litter where her father waited impatiently.

'You took your time, girl. What will I say to Silvanus if we are late?'

'I am sure you will have no trouble blaming it on me, Father,' Caecilia replied wearily.

Priscus screwed up his face with a disapproving frown. 'No wonder Antonius died so young if he had an insolent wife like you.'

'I would hardly have called Antonius young, Father. Certainly not in comparison to, say, Scipio.'

Her father's cheeks coloured and he glanced out of the litter. It was enough to let Caecilia know that Silvanus had been right – her next husband would be Scipio Marius. It was not such a bad choice, all things considered.

'If you are planning to marry me to Scipio, then why are we visiting Silvanus?' Caecilia asked.

Priscus kept his eyes averted, his hand nervously twitching the curtain of the litter. 'Silvanus is an influential trader. He supplies perfumes to the nobility of Rome as well as the provinces. He is a man to befriend.'

'From what I hear, he is a man to avoid,' Caecilia commented.

'Slaves' gossip,' Priscus said, sounding more evasive than dismissive. 'I want to discuss business with Silvanus, but, if you find his company too bitter to stomach, you may wait in a different room.'

The rest of the journey proceeded in silence, Caecilia becoming more anxious with every jolt of the litter. Was she letting her imagination run away with her? She had heard tales of bloodsucking demons in her own nursery

128

and hadn't believed them then. Yet now ... there was something about Silvanus. Staring into his eyes was like looking over the edge of the cliff; the drop was dizzying, frightening and enticing.

Silvanus' villa was on the Caelian Hill and set in lavish grounds. It glistened white in the late-afternoon sun, as if made entirely of marble. A muscular slave with bronzed skin met them in the atrium and Priscus announced, 'Your master knows I am coming. I will wait here to be received by him properly, but my daughter shall wait in another room. She will be no part of this.'

The slave looked at Caecilia with a boldness that unnerved her, but he inclined his head in obedience and led her into a small room where a jug of chilled wine and some sesame cakes had been laid out. Caecilia nibbled on one as she waited. By the time she had finished it, she was hot and bored. If her father wished her to have no part in the discussions, she may as well return home.

She stood up to leave but a figure stepped through the door. Silvanus. He wore a toga, but no tunic beneath it, and his skin gleamed with oil. Her fingers twitched with a sudden desire to trace the shimmering muscles of his chest. He came to stand before her with a smile and dark eyes. In the same way that a child knows to flee from a hissing snake, Caecilia knew that the man before her was a predator; one that could be swift and deadly, or could sport with you before making its kill.

'I am sorry to have kept you waiting, but I needed to see your father first,' Silvanus said with all civility. 'But I am now at leisure to speak with you while he is … entertained.'

The relish with which he said the last word sent a shiver down Caecilia's spine, but not an unpleasant one.

'So the rumours are true,' she said. 'Your home is one of sinful pleasure.'

'Are you suggesting that your father would visit such a place?' Silvanus teased, reaching past her for a sesame cake. He bit into it, his teeth appearing normal with no hint of the incisors she had seen.

'I am not blind to his ways, nor deaf to what I hear. We live in the reign of Tiberius, under the corrupt governance of Sejanus. Rome has a licence for lasciviousness. Many man mix business and pleasure, and my father is no different.'

Silvanus smiled. 'You are a unique woman, Caecilia. Somehow both worldly and beguilingly innocent. Any man would be lucky to have you by his side –' Silvanus stepped closer and Caecilia felt a familiar light-headedness '– or in his bed.'

He was so close, she could have fulfilled her desire to reach out and run her fingers over his skin. Her legs felt heavy and unwilling as she stepped away from him.

'Silvanus, the man of the forest,' she mused, trying to slow her frantically beating heart. 'A name with few hints in it as to its origin. Which forest, for example?'

Caecilia had been moving slowly about the room, as if admiring the décor. Silvanus, who had remained stationary, watching her, began to follow her movements, matching her step for step.

'I have visited many, in my time. I have lived so long, I forget which tree it was under which my mother first bore me and gave me that name.'

'You have lived long? How long?'

'Long enough to recognise a frightened young woman who has realised my true nature.'

Caecilia stopped; so did Silvanus. She turned to face him. She was frightened, yet intrigued. Every moment he did not attack her, she felt herself safer. And every moment she was near him, she felt her desire spiral higher.

'My slave talks of the Empusa,' she said, 'a creature that can transform itself into a beautiful woman. It seduces men, then drinks their blood while they sleep.'

'Slaves always have the most interesting and exotic tales, don't you think?' Silvanus said lazily.

He stepped a little closer. Caecilia stood her ground and would not be diverted.

'We have our own tales in Rome – the strigoi. Some think they are dead men walking, others whisper that they are witches with magical powers. All agree that they can turn into animals, make themselves hidden from human eyes and drink the blood of the living.'

Silvanus' eyes narrowed as he stepped closer still.

Caecilia felt like a mouse facing a prowling cat, but she did not flinch. Excitement was heating her blood, chasing away the chill of fear.

'If you know what I am, why come?' Silvanus asked curiously.

Boldly, Caecilia stepped forward, closing the distance between them to virtually nothing. Silvanus looked surprised.

'Because I dream about you,' Caecilia said, her voice little more than a whisper. 'It is never the same, but we are always making love. In some, I am covered in blood and you lick it off me with a cold but eager tongue. In others, you sink your teeth into my neck even as you plunge deep inside me. Both of them make me cry out in ecstasy.'

A hungry gleam had entered Silvanus' eyes. His tongue slid across his lips as he stared down at her. 'I have similar dreams,' he admitted, stepping so close she could feel his erection through their clothes.

Her heart jumped in anticipation. She brushed her hand against his hardness, marvelling at his girth against what she remembered of Antonius' weak efforts. He swallowed a groan and stepped away.

'I have had many names in my time, but my nature is unchanging,' he said, his voice husky with repressed desire. 'I need blood to survive, and I have my tricks to take it from the living. I can only take blood from a person three times before I must turn them into one of us or leave them to die. So it is well for you, little bird, that I am leaving tomorrow. You have proved by far the most tempting morsel in Rome.'

'You have fed from me twice?' Caecilia asked, baffled.

'No, only once, but –'

'Once is not three times.' Caecilia stepped forward, her hand snaking under his tunic faster than he could stop it. His shaft was warm and hard and she gripped it, squeezing and caressing as she spoke. 'I will be married to Scipio soon. He may prove a more enticing husband than Antonius, he may not. Another time would only make it twice that you have fed on me, and I am willing to give you what you need freely in return for what I want.'

This time, Silvanus could not prevent his groan from escaping. His hand caught her wrist, pulling her from him, but his eyes shone with desire. 'Very well then,' he growled. 'Come with me, little bird.'

Still holding her wrist, he led her across the atrium and into another room, low lit and filled with incense. Shadows squirmed around her, and as her eyes accustomed she released they were men and women engaging in a variety of carnal activities. The gloom was too great for her to make out the people, but her heart fluttered in her chest as Silvanus hurried them through. It was impossible to tell whether the cries and groans were ones of pain or pleasure, or if any of them belonged to her father.

Silvanus led her through another door into an empty

room. He turned and grinned at her wolfishly. 'So, now that we are here, little bird, do you still have the stomach for it? To make love to a monster?'

In answer, Caecilia reached up, unpinned her tunic and let it fall to the floor. When the cool air touched her sex, she realised just how wet and ready she was. Silvanus' gaze swept over her and her nipples hardened beneath the lust in his eyes. In a few swift movements, he discarded his own garments. They stood for a moment, facing each other. Silvanus' chest heaved with deep breaths as he regarded his prey, and Caecilia's arousal was almost unbearable as she took in his lithe form. Then, with the speed of a wild animal, he was upon her.

He swept her round, tugging her towards the bed which stood against the wall. He pushed her down on to the cool sheets and was instantly on top of her. Caecilia cried out in a mixture of pain and pleasure as his thick shaft parted and stretched her sex. Despite his urgency, he slid inside her slowly, giving her time to accommodate all of him.

When every inch of him was inside her, he bent his head to suck on her nipples. His tongue caressed them and his teeth tugged at them until she was gasping for him to stop. Not once had he moved within her but the feel of him was excruciatingly teasing. As he pulled his head away, she pulled her hips back so that he slid out of her a little way, then rocked them forward so that she sank down on him again. He arched his back, lifting his weight off her so she could move more freely. She writhed eagerly beneath him while he remained motionless above her.

He lowered his head, planting hungry kisses on her chin, her shoulder, her neck. Wrapping her legs around him, Caecilia drove him deeper inside her with every thrust of her hips. She could feel the orgasm building within her when a sharp pain lanced across her shoulder and down her arm as Silvanus sank his teeth into her. Yet, even as she cried out, the pain faded to be replaced by a powerful burning in her blood. She rocked her hips harder beneath him, straining to engulf as much of him as possible.

Silvanus threw his head back, his lips red and a thin line of blood trickling down his chin. He licked his lips then looked down, meeting Caecilia's eyes. He began to move within her, matching her hip thrusts with her own. Caecilia wrapped her legs tighter around his waist, her nails digging into his back and drawing blood of her own.

She crested her orgasm once, then tumbled into it again as Silvanus continued to ride her hard. The world blurred with pleasure and she thought Silvanus would never stop thrusting into her, but then he stiffened as he reached his own peak. He slumped, panting hard. When he smiled down at her, she saw that his two incisors had grown longer than his other teeth. She leaned up and kissed him passionately before they had to part.

* * *

When Priscus finally returned to the room where he had left his daughter, he found Caecilia sitting quietly, reading a book she had evidently acquired from somewhere. 'I am sorry, my dear. Business took longer than I thought,' he said, adjusting his crumpled toga. 'I hope you were not too bored?'

Caecilia put down her book and smiled contentedly. 'Not at all, Father. I managed to amuse myself in your absence. Are you ready to leave?'

'Indeed. I'm famished. Let us return and see what Tychon has ready for our dinner. But a moment – your necklace is askew.'

Caecilia reached up, pulling the thick gold choker back into position, trying not to wince as it rubbed the raw skin beneath. 'Thank you, Father. I think I'm perfectly ready to go home now.'

V-Positive
Teresa Noelle Roberts

'Leona,' I said, 'you're the hottest woman I've met in a long time.' Maybe ever, but that sounded pathetic, given what I had to say next. 'But I'm not human.'

'You're human,' she responded coolly. Her grey eyes stayed locked with mine. 'You just have the V. I know I'm not looking at a Goth chick with funky contacts. Your fangs show if you're not careful when you smile. But you're still human.'

Time for the long version of the speech. 'If you analyse my DNA, it's almost human, but not quite. I'm not just me any more. I'm me plus a mutagenic virus that's turned me into this blood-drinking *thing*. The only foods I can digest, other than blood, are oysters and dark chocolate, which is better than parsnips and sauerkraut would be, but even chocolate gets old if that's all you can eat. But that's not the bad part. The bad part is the cravings. We want human blood. All the time. We want to pass the virus along to those who feed us. All the time. We're nocturnal predators. That's why they call us vampires, even if they know it's a mutated space-virus and not Dracula rising from his grave. I can keep the impulses at bay most of the time, but sex makes it harder to hold them off. And I don't want to harm you, or anyone else for that matter. So no sex with the uninfected.'

And no sex with the infected either, at least not unless I met an infected woman who was kinky in the right ways. I may be a predatory freak with a contagious mutagenic disease, but I have standards.

I finished my speech. I expected Leona to look hurt, concerned, scared, maybe defiant and ready to insist that love or at least lust would conquer all. Instead, she simply stared at me, her grey eyes flat and inscrutable and, I thought, almost as predatory as mine on a bad night, though it was obvious from her rosy cheeks and normal, non-reflective eyes she didn't have the V.

'So that's why I can't possibly date you, even though I'd like to,' I added lamely, looking away from those intense eyes.

I've been a shy, subby femme equally aroused and unnerved by a hot butch for a lot longer than I've been a fierce nocturnal predator, and, on my good nights, the inner shy bottom is actually in control, not the thing with fangs and a bad attitude.

But I have bad nights, just like everyone with the V does, nights when I'm just a virus looking for a host, a hungry animal looking for prey. I didn't want Leona, with her short red hair and her neatly pressed men's button-down shirts and her lovely, slightly scary grey eyes, to be around when I had a bad night. Maybe outside my front door, locking me in, because she looked determined enough to resist my pleas to be let out and tough enough not to freak, but not near me. Certainly not in my bed.

Even though my core self and my inner predator both wanted her in that bed.

And the wanting was mutual. One of the interesting effects of V is a selectively improved sense of smell. Specifically, we're aware of pheromones on a much more conscious level than healthy humans are, and we can smell arousal before the person has admitted to herself that she's interested. I guess it's so the virus can find new hosts more easily, but I wish I'd had this ability when it was still safe to follow up on it.

Because, damn, Leona was having a party in her panties and she wanted me to co-host.

I could smell how much she wanted me, even though her face was cool, impassive, distant, as if I hadn't just spilled my heart to her. As if she hadn't been the one to ask me out for a beer she must have known I couldn't drink and then propositioned me.

Even though I'd just told her all the very good reasons

I'd never kiss her full lips, never caress the small firm breasts that her tailored shirt couldn't quite hide, never learn if her sensible, short-nailed hand would fit inside my cunt or how she wielded a strap-on.

'Say something,' I finally begged, unable to stand the silence and that unnerving stare another second. 'I'm sorry. I hate having to turn you down.'

'Some predator. I can see you stalking your prey down a midnight street – then viciously demanding a heart-to-heart and snuggles.'

I couldn't help laughing because Leona was right. But it suggested she hadn't gotten the point of what I'd said earlier. 'Rose Perry cries at mushy movies and has had the urge to show up with a moving van on the second date. But I'm not just Rose Perry any more. I'm me plus the V, and the V is bad-ass even if I'm not. I have fangs, Leona. I can bench-press a car. OK, a Mini, but that's still not something humans should be able to do. And, even while the human part of me is thinking how cute you'd look in my bathrobe tomorrow morning with a goofy post-sex grin on your face, the V knows what blood type you are and wonders how you'd taste and if you'd freak out or come when I bit you. It doesn't care which you'd do, although coming is better because that means you might let me have seconds.'

'I know all that,' Leona purred. 'It's what makes you hot.' She stood up, stalked around the table – damn, she did the predator stalk better than I did – and stood disarmingly close to me. I could smell her arousal, smell her blood, hear her pulse. 'You're a soft, sweet girl with a predator inside – and you want that predator controlled in the worst way.'

I was dripping wet, wondering how those small, strong-looking hands would feel on my breasts, wondering how her cunt-juices would taste.

Wondering how her skin would part beneath my fangs. She was type A positive. I could smell that as sharply as I could her lust.

'Go away, Leona,' I growled. 'You're turning me on, and it's not safe.' As I said it, I stood and lurched towards her like a drunk. The V wanted me to and, because I also wanted to, all the common sense on earth couldn't stop me.

But Leona could.

Before I knew it, I had handcuffs clamped around my wrists. Not cute fur-lined play cuffs, but the specially reinforced kind cops use when someone with the V runs amuck.

This would explain why Leona wanted to meet me in a bar that was a meeting place for the local leather community. I'd assumed it was for the great beer selection (none of which I could taste, alas) but I guess she'd hoped our conversation might reach the point where the cuffs were needed. At the Back Room, no one would look twice.

141

OK, they'd look twice, but only if they enjoyed the view.

'I know it's risky,' Leona purred in my ear, frustratingly out of reach. 'I like risky. And you must hate being too dangerous to love. What if I say I can make it safe for you to enjoy sex again, Rose?'

I sputtered. It took me a while to do something more than sputter because her words, her smell and the cuffs were conspiring against my brain. Back when I used to have sex, I always had a thing for a top who'd take charge when I wasn't expecting it.

What about my inner predator, the big scary fanged creature hidden inside my skin?

Damn if the thing wasn't ready to roll over, expose its belly, and wriggle blissfully, or whatever an alpha bitch did when it met something more alpha than it was.

Finally, my brain kicked back into action, probably because my baser instincts, both human and virus-driven, desperately wanted to believe she had an answer for me, a way that I could enjoy touching, fucking, even something as simple as kissing, again. 'How?'

'Handcuffs,' Leona purred. 'And rope. Lots and lots of lovely hemp rope. A latex outfit and pretty latex gloves so I can touch you but your virus can't touch me. And a knife handy, just in case. What do you say, Rose?'

I think I opened and closed my mouth a few times without making a sound, trying to figure out how she'd read my mind. Then I nodded, still silent, but enthusiastic.

'You really should have deleted your FetLife profile if you were serious about celibacy, beautiful,' Leona whispered. 'Bill told me your user name. He's a sweet boy, and he worries about you being lonely. Besides, he wanted to take this hot guy to Allegro and I had a gift certificate.'

Yeah, that sounded like my ex-roommate: misguided but sweet, and easily bribed by shiny objects.

Leona clipped a leash on to the bit of sturdy chain that connected the cuffs. My panties flooded. A quivering began in my lower belly.

'Are we going?' she asked, but it wasn't really a question. She was leading me out of the bar before I found the breath to whisper my *yes*.

The bartender applauded as we headed out. He hadn't heard the conversation, but clearly approved the show.

I could have escaped. I'd have been stuck in the cuffs for a while, but I'm faster and stronger than any uninfected human, and, once the mutations kick in, a lot less inhibited by normal rules about not hurting innocent bystanders.

Luckily, I didn't want to escape. Not even the inner beast wanted to get away. Nor did it want to attack Leona, at least not in non-fun, non-consensual senses of the word *attack*. The beast was curiously quiet for the ride to her duplex, not dormant, but content as that part of me rarely was. If it had been a cat, it would have purred. Loudly and with an edge of danger, like a happy tiger, but a purr is a purr.

I assume Leona had furniture, but all I saw was the bondage frame in what, in someone else's house, would be the living room.

It was black and super-sturdy, like you could suspend a truck from it, let alone a person. On the other side of the room, there was a cage that looked like it once held lions for transport to a zoo.

'You've given this a lot of thought.' It crossed my mind to say *you're kinky for V-positive people*, but I didn't, for the basest of reasons. She was insanely sexy and, if she was fascinated by the V, I was benefiting from it.

'There's no greater turn-on than dominating and controlling someone strong who chooses to be weak for me. If it's someone who could overpower me easily, someone dangerous, it's hotter.'

I understood this from the flip side. It was an amazing head-fuck to feel this helpless, this yielding before someone I could probably crush like a bug and whose human life I could certainly destroy. I could overpower her, but, for the moment, she ruled me by sheer force of will.

With my hands cuffed, Leona had to help me get undressed. Slithering my long black skirt off was easy, but the little bit of contact left me trembling. It had been so long.

To get my blouse off, she used a knife.

I held very still as she delicately destroyed the lace and satin. (Hey, if you have V, you might as well go for the Victorian Goth look. At least at first glance people think you look funky and sexy instead of dangerous and scary.) I didn't speak, didn't move, didn't breathe. I couldn't afford to bleed. The virus had to stay contained inside my skin.

The knife committed its intimate destruction without grazing me. At the end, though, when the blouse hung in tatters, exposing me to her gaze, she let the cold flat of the blade slip lightly over my skin and I melted.

Leona had control over herself. Leona had control over me.

I'd felt out of control ever since Bill called 911 in a panic because he thought I was dead. (I heard every terrified-twink shriek; V-positive people can be shaken out of our daytime coma by loud noises, but we still can't move or react.) I'd spent months being pushed around by a bunch of microscopic pathogens that were destroying my life and using me to destroy others – utterly without malice, just intent on their own survival, and all the more implacable for that.

Now, in Leona's hands, I felt safe. I didn't have to try to stay in control and fail. Leona was taking care of it.

The virus prompted me to struggle a few times as she tied me up, but I let Leona know when it was happening and she'd grab the back of my neck hard or lay the flat of the knife between my breasts. The predator recognised one of its own kind and submitted. Or maybe my own need to yield was so fierce it overwhelmed the predator.

Leona had chosen a deep-red hemp rope, beautiful against my V-pale skin. She'd obviously washed it a few times, so it was firm yet soft, like the coarse caress of a wool sweater. I hadn't felt rope on my skin for far too long, since before V. It made me feel contained, embraced – safe. Each coil of the rope restrained me a little more, and the more restrained I was, the safer I felt. When I went half-limp in the bonds, she uncuffed me, moved my hands behind my back and cuffed me again. I didn't even think to fight.

I wound up in one of those positions that make you pity the model in a bondage photo shoot: balanced on one leg, the other out to the side at a ninety-degree angle and supported by a lot of rope. Rope corseted my body as well, wrapped my breasts, pulled my pussy lips even more open than the position forced them, kept my cuffed hands snug behind my back. In the end, even my hair was bound. She braided rope into it and attached the rope to the frame.

Pre-V, I'd have been lucky to last five minutes in this position before something cramped hideously and I needed to safeword. Now I was stronger, with the balance and flexibility of a yogini and the inner stillness of a predator stalking her prey. Now there was no discomfort to distract me from the fact I was utterly, deliciously immobilised by a beautiful top's red rope, nothing to take away from the wonder of being wet and open under her gaze.

This was the bondage experience I'd sought time and again when I was still human and couldn't achieve for more than a few glorious minutes before my body or mind pulled me out of bliss by reminding me of discomfort. Now there was only the bliss.

I could have snapped the ropes, but the euphoria I was experiencing bled over to the predator. I got the sense that, to my mutated self, Leona was a fellow predator, but of an unknown kind. Something to treat with respect, something to watch closely.

Something that was definitely not prey, but might be a mate.

Leona tucked in the last rope end and kissed me.

I kept my mouth stubbornly closed, despite the temptation of those delicious lips. Scientists had determined the V wasn't transmitted through kissing alone, but, if her tongue slipped into my mouth, I might not be able to resist the urge to bite it and that would transmit my saliva right into Leona's blood, chancing contagion.

'You won't bite me,' she whispered, her lips grazing mine. 'I forbid it.' Leona's small hand grasped my face, urging my mouth open.

I melted. Maybe the part of me that wasn't exactly me melted too, or maybe it was too stunned by Leona's authority to react with violence. My lips parted. Her tongue slipped between them.

She let it touch my fangs.

I wanted to bite down. My whole body quivered to bite down, all the mutated bits of me screaming for her delicious blood.

But, after a second, the mutations were screaming just as loudly not to bite her. Leona didn't smell stupid. Leona smelled confident. If she smelled that confident when she knew she was teasing a predator, she was scary-dangerous herself.

My inner predator thought scary was just as sexy as I did.

For the first time since I was diagnosed, I kissed a woman with passion, and that was enough to have me quivering in my bonds. My spread-open cunt throbbed. I tried to arch so my body could press against Leona's, but I couldn't, not secured as I was.

Feeling myself straining against the ropes, I felt that much safer. Even if I went completely V-mad, it would be work to break out of all those feet of strong rope, and that would buy Leona enough time to get away.

By the time she pulled away, I was panting and moisture dripped down my thighs.

'Stay where you are, beautiful,' she teased, and

sauntered out of the room as only a butch top who'd just finished tying up a lover she wanted to torment further could saunter.

It seemed she was gone a year and a day, but it also seemed no time passed at all before she returned, dressed in skin-tight black latex pants and a matching top – and the promised long red latex gloves. A thick red strap-on thrust into the air in front of her as she approached me. Her throat sported a steel collar, which she pointed to with one latex-covered finger. 'Not my usual style,' she joked, 'but it should make you think twice about going for my jugular. You wouldn't want to chip your pretty fangs.'

I struggled for words, but I couldn't find them. Mesmerised, I watched her silicone cock bob and weave as she approached. My hands strained against the steel that confined them, wanting to touch her, but they weren't going anywhere without my letting the mutations take complete control and going all Nosferatu on Leona.

Since no one in their right mind would want to fuck Nosferatu and I really, really wanted to get fucked, I stayed put.

And Leona thrust into me.

My body offered no resistance, the proverbial hot knife and soft butter.

I'm not usually the kind of girl who comes from penetration alone. I love the way it feels, but it doesn't take me over the edge. Penetration plus lots of rope plus an incredibly hot woman in latex plus the end of my longest period of celibacy since I was sixteen – that was another story. My cunt started contracting around that silicone dick almost instantly and I started kissing and licking at any part of Leona I could reach.

Licking and kissing, but not biting, because the latex smell masked the scent of her blood, the flavour of her skin.

Full-body latex is one of the ways V-positive people can have sex halfway safely, but most people, no matter what their V status, are just not that into being cased in a substance that looks sexy, but tastes like a day at the dentist and has a texture you either love or hate.

Lucky for me, I'm kinky for latex. And lucky for Leona, the virus apparently evolved in a place that didn't have latex, so the mutated bits of me didn't react to that wonderful smell with the excitement that I did.

Leona was a latex-clad goddess restoring my world. She was fucking me senseless and the virus hardly registered her presence for the very reason I found her so irresistible.

Fairly soon, though, I lost the ability even to kiss with any coordination, because I was too busy coming. It only got worse, which is to say better, when Leona slipped a latex-clad hand between us that was applying pressure to both our clits.

I lost track of time. I lost track of how often I came. I lost track of my own name. Everything in the universe dwindled to the ropes that embraced me and kept Leona safe, and to the woman fucking me, her body pressed against mine, so confident in her rope work and her own dominant power that she didn't fear me.

By the time Leona slipped out of me, I hung limp against the ropes and I think I was babbling. I heard the thud as she dropped the strap-on to the floor, but I was past looking up.

I was still riding the euphoria, twitching with aftershocks of pleasure, when I felt a tug, followed by a sudden, unwelcome sense of release. After all the exquisite care she'd taken to rig me into bondage, Leona was freeing me simply by cutting the ropes. Without their support, even the V couldn't keep me standing and I sank to the floor, my hands still bound behind me.

'We're not done yet. Get over here,' Leona ordered, pointing to the floor between her legs. I did my best to comply, but I couldn't manage to stand on my jelly legs and couldn't crawl with my hands behind my back. Still, I couldn't stop myself from trying to obey. She chuckled a bit when she realised my conundrum, but her hands were exquisitely gentle as she helped me up to my knees and stood over me.

'Let's try that again, shall we?' she asked, her voice gentler this time, but still holding a tone of command.

'Fucking you was great, but I need more. Lick me, Rose. Lick me through the latex.'

'Jesus, do you have any idea what you're asking?' My voice trembled with fear, with desire, with awe at the trust she was putting in me. Latex had kept the V at bay so far, but what would happen if I could feel the heat of her cunt, hear the blood pulse in her clit? The taste of latex would arouse me even more. Even if my mutant passenger didn't appreciate the allure of latex, it certainly understood the uses of lust. 'I'm not sure I have that much self-control.'

'Good thing I have control for both of us.'

She'd left the ropes in my braid. Now I knew why. She gathered the rope and the braid itself into one hand, ready to yank my head away if need be.

The other hand held the knife she'd used to cut the ropes.

She rested it on the side of my neck. I'm pretty sure it was the flat of the blade but I couldn't swear to it. 'I don't want to use this for anything except teasing,' she said. 'But I bet knowing it's there will keep you in line.'

What it did was make me into something small and malleable and even wetter than I had been, which I didn't think possible.

'Lick,' she ordered, and I did.

I tasted myself. I tasted latex. I couldn't taste Leona, would never be able to taste Leona directly because that would make it almost impossible to resist biting her. But I heard her moans, felt her rolling her pelvis as I licked, sensed as her body froze and then released with the explosion of orgasm.

I felt when she let the knife clatter to the floor, felt it when the death-grip on my hair loosened.

I could have bitten then. By that time, I could smell her juices, smell her heat, and that could have overcome the V's aversion to latex.

But, by that time, I couldn't harm her because it would have meant disobeying her.

In the end, when she pushed me away because she couldn't take any more pleasure just then, I stayed kneeling at her feet, leaning against her leg like a cat or dog.

A domesticated predator.

'It's nearly dawn,' she said, stroking my hair. 'I wish I could curl up with you until then, but it's probably not a good idea. If I start to drift off …'

'Yeah.' If the force of Leona's personality was masked by sleep, I wasn't sure I could resist biting her. 'I'll go home, I guess.'

'Stay in the guest room. We'll hang out until dawn comes. I have tomorrow off so I can sleep in.'

And we did. Leona sat in a chair next to the guest bed holding my hand and we talked until the sunrise I couldn't see through heavy blinds started to take its toll.

My speech slurred. My eyelids twitched. I tried to fight it, but they shut despite my best efforts.

My breathing slowed to the point where it would be imperceptible to most people. My skin, I knew, was growing cold.

Before I lost touch with the daylight world I'd never see again, I felt the bed shift as Leona settled down beside me. She kissed my forehead like you might kiss a child. 'I'll see you at sunset, Rose,' she whispered. 'I'll pick up some plasma at the pharmacy for you, and spend the rest of the day coming up with new ways for us to play.'

I drifted into the daylight coma with a smile that let my fangs show.

Death by V
Chrissie Bentley

The break room of the Public Library isn't the kind of place you'd normally expect to meet a vampire, even if you were looking for one. Which, I want to make very clear, I was not. Yes, I'd spent my teens embroiled within precisely the same cultural reference points as the rest of my generation – Sookie Stackhouse, Anne Rice and *Twilight* – and, I suppose, if I ever had the time to take one of those self-professedly 'scarily accurate' quizzes on Facebook, 'who is your ideal date', Henry Fitzroy would be in the Top Five.

But that's about as far as my thoughts on the subject went, and they were still there that wet January evening when I was finally relieved from my seat at the checkout desk, made my way past the two or three homeless guys that appear to be our most regular customers, tutted at the teenagers who were trying to call up some porn on the computers, and finally slumped into what passed for a comfortable chair with my back to the soft-drinks-dispensing machine.

Sheba looked up as I sat down. 'I bet you'll be glad when this shift is over?'

I nodded. The last few days before school resumes are always difficult, as the building fills with panicked kids finally remembering what their summer projects were, and falling over themselves to get it started now. And, if the days are bad, the evenings are even worse. It's funny, remembering back to my childhood, the library at night was always a magical place, silent enough that your imagination could run riot, but bright enough to keep the shadows in check. Books felt more alluring at night as well; as soon as you entered the building, you could hear them whispering and calling you, inviting you to take them home and read them through until morning.

I kept those memories for a long time as well, tucked away safely among my favourite things, so it struck me as something of a personal triumph when I landed a job in those same mystic hours. A triumph that lasted for at least the first ten minutes of my first evening on duty, when I saw my first drunk throw up on the carpet beside my station. It was cleaned up quickly enough, of course, but the smell lingered for the rest of my shift, to be joined by – in no particular order – urine, faeces, fast food and some of the foulest aftershave I've ever encountered. I was leered at more times than I could remember, pawed at least twice and given such a hard time by one middle-aged man that I came close to calling security.

Since then ... since then, I've grown accustomed to all those things and worse, but there's something about back-to-school time that makes everything else feel like a mere preamble.

'Still, it's only a few days,' I finally answered, and it was her turn to nod, a signal not only that she agreed with me, but also that the conversation was at an end.

I thought back to when she started work here, a month ago give or take a few days. It was as though she'd just appeared from nowhere; nobody seemed to remember her being introduced to the rest of us, nobody knew when she'd been interviewed or even who she replaced. She was just there, sitting in the break room with a bottle of tomato juice, and, although every one of us tried to make conversation, or at least respond to something she said, the exchange never survived more than a couple of sentences. Then she'd nod and return to the book she was reading.

* * *

Out on the floor, too, she was silent. Questions from the public – and looking the way she did, she got a lot of them usually from adolescent boys and lonely-looking middle-aged men – would be answered as briskly as possible, and then she'd hurry away in another direction entirely, and no matter where you thought she was standing the last place you saw her, the next time she'd be someplace else entirely.

But management seemed happy with her, and, when the suggestions box was emptied every Saturday, she was the only one on the entire staff who wasn't the subject of at least one complaint. Or, strangely enough, one suggestion. Everybody noticed her, everybody tried to speak to her. But nobody, not even the horniest High School kid on a dare from his buddies, ever even dreamed of actually interacting with her.

With my nose in *Vanity Fair*, but my eyes skimming just above the page, I studied her for a moment – the dark hair that threatened to turn to curls, but contented itself with a bob instead; the deep-brown eyes that were big enough to hold your attention, but not so large that she looked like a cow; the mouth that always looked like it wanted to smile, but couldn't quite decide whether anything deserved that ... and you could carry on like that for the rest of her body, every feature of her frame poised in gorgeous indecision. She was neither tall nor short, large-chested nor small, well dressed nor casual. And, though she was certainly beautiful, even that issue was slightly clouded – she wasn't a movie star, but she wasn't the girl next door, either. She was simply Sheba.

'Sorry, did you say something?' Suddenly she was looking right at me, although I knew she hadn't moved her head.

I collected my thoughts as fast as I could. 'No. Sorry, I was staring, wasn't I? I was just wondering where you got those earrings?' There was some truth to that as well; I'd noticed them when she arrived for work this evening, cut-out silver hieroglyphs that may or may not have had diamond insets.

She laughed. 'A little place in Cairo,' she answered, as casually as if she was talking about the flea market in Fremont. She was silent for a moment, and then: 'It's probably not there any longer. Shame, they had some nice things.'

I sensed an opening. 'Have you travelled much?'

She slammed her book shut. 'Here and there.'

'Do they mean anything? The hieroglyphs?'

'Probably not.'

Another silence, which I thought of breaking with the story of a friend of mine who happily wore a pair of gorgeous Chinese letters in her ears until a co-worker, a Chinese woman who just happened to be her boss, suggested that walking around with the words 'fuck me' hanging from her head maybe wasn't a statement she intended to make. I wasn't certain that Sheba would see the humour in it anyway, so I kept quiet, and then jumped when she broke the silence.

'You're Chrissie, aren't you?'

'Yeah.'

'I'm sorry, I'm terrible with names. Have you worked here long?'

'Nearly a year ...'

And suddenly we were just chatting away, about the job, about the customers, about our fellow staff, and I was just about to bend the topic towards her own background when she glanced at the clock above the break-room door and sighed, 'I'd better be going. My break ended five minutes ago.'

'Oh, God, I'm sorry.'

'Don't worry about it. I doubt whether anybody's noticed anyway.' She poured what remained of her drink down the sink, ran the tap to flush it away, then stepped towards the door. 'Are you doing anything after work?'

'I don't think so. No, no I'm not.'

'I was just wondering if you wanted to go for a drink? Wash away what's left of this evening?'

Through the door that she held half open, I could hear the shrieks and laughter of a bunch of High Schoolers going out of their way to disobey the library's code of conduct. She was right, it was the kind of evening you just wanted to forget.

'Yeah, that'd be fun. Shall we ask any of the others along?'

She hesitated for a moment. But finally she spoke. 'Well, you could if you really want to,' she said, but her tone of voice left me in no doubt what she really thought of my suggestion, so I smiled and said, 'Not really,' and we agreed to meet back there at ten.

I would be lying if I said there wasn't a tiny cloud clinging to the back of my mind as I walked back to my work station and psyched myself up for the next three hours of mundane questions, idiot responses and surly demands. I knew nothing about Sheba beyond what she'd volunteered during our conversation. Nothing about her home life, nothing about her friends and relationships, nothing about her background, and nothing whatsoever about her reasons for asking me out for a drink, and making it so clear that she wanted us to be alone.

Was she gay? The possibility was certainly there and, while it didn't bother me in itself, there was a dark corner in my mind which wondered whether that was the only reason she'd shown any interest in me, because she hoped for some kind of sexual encounter. Which – and I was surprised at just how vehemently my mind dismissed the possibility – she was not going to get. Theoretically, I get it – what is sex anyway, beyond an extension of friendship, which itself is a far more intimate relationship than being lovers. A meeting of the minds touches you to every depth of your being; a meeting of the bodies is simply that, a physical encounter that can be washed away the next time you shower. That I understand, and I believe it too.

At the same time, though, would I actually want to go through with it? With the physical mechanics of sex with another woman, even if she was my best friend? Even as I congratulated myself for being the first person in the building to get past Sheba's outer defences, I was certain that I wouldn't want to penetrate too much deeper. The question was, did she want me to? Well, we'd find out later, when I discovered where she was intending us to go. If it was a lesbian hangout, I'd know for sure.

In fact, she didn't have any place in mind. We just walked around the corner from the library and into the first open doorway we found, one of those faux-Irish joints which every neighbourhood seems to attract, and where the clientele is neatly divided between the regular drinkers and passing trade. Certainly, we weren't the only people who'd obviously stopped off on our way home from one job or another, and it surprised me just how many gigs there were these days that kept their employees out until the end of the evening.

But we found a booth that wasn't too noisy, ordered drinks from a bored college boy with a beard, and more or less picked up our conversation from where we'd left off. A few more work-related observations, a handful of non-committal comments on life in general, just a couple of workmates hanging out in their spare time. As I walked back to my apartment at the end of the night – how lucky I am to have a job just ten minutes away from where I live – I was almost disappointed that Sheba hadn't made a pass at me. At least I'd know *something* about her.

* * *

Three weeks later, I know more than I could ever have imagined. Beginning with the fact that she's a vampire.

I know what you're thinking, because I thought it as well. But then I thought about it and figured that the old legends had to start somewhere, and then I asked her about it and I learned that the old legends were wrong to begin with.

Very, very wrong. And you can ask Charlie Trachori if you don't believe me. He was in the same bar that night that Sheba and I had our first date, and, oh, God, I groaned when I first saw him watching us. Because there's certain words that I rarely use to describe another human being, but there's one that fits Charlie T to a tee. And his parents figured it out on his first day in the world, even if it did take them eight more months to realise their mistake; eight months during which little Charlie happily gurgled, widdled and squirmed his way through their proud-as-Punch world, and not a shadow crossed anybody's mind. Not, that is, until his mother had stitched the final bar of the final letter of baby's first monogrammed outfit, paused, and then screamed for her husband. Really screamed.

163

It was all his fault, of course. His fault for insisting that Charlie be named for both of his grandfathers, and his fault for insisting that his own dad came first. Charles Ulysses Nelson Trachori sounded so grand on the birth announcements, and it rolled so sweetly off the tongue. But it was an acronymical viper and Mama had just been bitten. From that day forth, little Charlie had no middle names whatsoever and, if, as the boy grew into a man, his playmates renamed him Connecticut, that was a small price to pay compared with what they might have been calling him.

Sticks and stones. Names cannot hurt but they can prove oddly prescient. Into adulthood, into business, and Charlie Trachori might as well have retained his grandparents' names. For they would at least have given early warning to his business partners, or the growing mound of figurative corpses that he scrambled across on his way to the top. At twenty-one, he was rising up the family business; at thirty-one, he was poised on the brink of assuming full control. And on the day of his thirty-fifth birthday, with one marriage behind him, two kids around him and at least four former employees gunning for his guts, he was holding forth to the platoon of sycophants with whom he most happily surrounded himself, reminding them again just how fabulous he was. Every one of them agreed with him.

It was Harrison who saw Sheba first, and I bet he

saw the same as everyone else does. She was standing by the bar, taller than most of the women in the place, and bustier as well. But that wasn't what drew the eye towards her. It was her eyes, dark ponds of eternity that he knew he shouldn't have been able to see from that far across the darkened room, but which he swam in regardless. She was so far out of his league, though, he knew that even before she broke the lingering gaze upon which she'd impaled him, and fixed it instead on the head of his table.

Harrison turned to look at Charlie. He was in the midst – he was always in the midst – of a long drawn-out tale in which his heroic role was outlined from the moment he let slip the first word. A barmaid whom he'd so generously tipped, who spent the next twenty minutes thanking him for it; the employee he'd fired but not without first promising to top up the old boy's retirement fund. Of course, he wouldn't do it – the only thing that came cheaper than promises to Trachori were the imported goods that he sold at top dollar to the most gullible boutique stores his ad team could con. But, for the ten minutes that the old man stood before his desk, Trachori bathed in such fulsome praise and compliment that you could almost understand why he had such a high opinion of himself. People really did seem to go out of their way to catch his eye.

Catch his eye. A movement to his left brought his

train of thought to a temporary halt; it was nothing, but he used the interruption to flag the waiter for another bottle of something expensive, and that's when he caught sight of Sheba.

He smiled to himself, and I knew what he was thinking. There were two types of woman in his world. The ones who did what he told them to, and the ones whom he told what to do. But they all had one thing in common. They could sense success, they could sniff out power, and Sheba had a nose like a bloodhound. They'd not even made eye contact and she was smiling at him, and not that general 'Hey, how are ya?' kind of smile that preambled most introductions. This was a deep smile, an intimate one, the sort of smile you'd sometimes have to spend a good few hundred bucks to get, and she'd still be expecting a ring on her finger. He smiled back, then raised his glass with the universal gesture of the rich and powerful. 'Join me,' it shouted. 'And if this isn't the most expensive wine you've ever tasted, I'll be very surprised.'

Sheba raised her eyebrows slightly, but didn't move. But her gaze still held him and her smile never wavered, and it was all Charlie could do to tear his eyes away from that perfect face, and check out the rest of the merchandise too.

Her expression followed his roving inspection, and was it his imagination or did her flesh – and her dress left a lot of it open to the sky – ripple gently as his eyes swept across it, as though his touch was already driving her insane? Did her breath hitch and her bosom heave, as though she were a Gothic romance princess, as his mind's eye caressed the best tits he'd seen all evening? Did she shift her stance and part her legs slightly as she felt his interest shift a little lower?

No, it wasn't his imagination. He stood and he'd have sworn that she was already on her knees before him, even though she was still on the far side of the room. Confident his voice would carry across the conversational hums that separated him from her, and confident, too, that nobody else would even dream of thinking he was talking to them, he called to her to join him, and this time she did, mouthing a faint 'See you later' to me, and then parting the crowd as she passed through the bar room, not even appearing to notice as perspiring businessmen and middle-aged spread-sheeters weaved and ducked their way out of her path. Even Charlie looked impressed as he watched her walk towards him, and he didn't even need to say a word; both of the bodies that sat closest to him vacated their seats so that she might sit there, and one even extinguished his cigarette.

He filled the glass that a hovering waiter had already placed before her, and awaited her first gasp of delight. She delivered it on cue, tasting the wine and then opening her eyes wide to look at him with what he knew was amazement. *Who are you*, he could imagine her mind asking, *who can offer me something against which even my beauty pales?* Because he knew that she knew she was lovely – in fact, at this moment he was certain that he'd never seen any woman so beautiful as ...

* * *

'What's your name?' he asked.

'Sheba,' she answered softly, the word shaped ever so slightly by an accent he immediately pegged as European. He didn't worry about narrowing in any further; he had no doubt that, by morning, he'd know all that he needed to about her life and times, the world to which she was born, and that to which she dreamed she might ascend, because that was another thing all women had in common. It didn't matter how proudly they carried themselves, it was what he carried in his wallet that they really wanted, and he knew when it came time to pay this night's expenses, she'd be as impressed by the size of the tip he would leave as the waiter who'd chase him out on to the street, thanking him profusely for his kind generosity. It would probably feed the man's family for the rest of the month.

Sheba was speaking. 'And yours?'

Charlie smiled. 'Charlie Trachori.' He paused while the last name sank in, then nodded when he guessed she was about to ask. *The* Charlie Trachori? One and the same. That was how his evenings usually went, and he had often wondered if he'd ever get bored with the babes swooning and gasping when they learned who he was. Maybe he would. But he hadn't yet, and so the evening wore on and the two of them talked until it was indeed time for this party to end, and for another to kick off back at –

'My place?' he asked casually.

'No, mine,' she replied, and he was shocked for a moment because most girls were gagging to see the mansion they'd all read about. Not Sheba, though, and he shuddered a little at the thought of what her own place might be like; small and poky, he was sure, with girlish décor and cute little knickknacks. He hoped it was at least in a decent part of town.

It was. In fact, as Charlie's driver pulled up by the perimeter gates, and Sheba gave him the code to open the lock, Charlie wondered if he'd misjudged the woman altogether. Well, not misjudged her, because he never did that. But maybe underestimated her a little. He wished she'd given a last name as well, and he scoured the database of local wealth that his mother had drummed into him as a child, in search of some kind of clue. But the car was inside the gardens now, and Sheba was already pointing the driver towards a light in the lower part of the house, where he might find her own staff having a nightcap.

'Will you be needing me to wait, sir?'

Charlie thought for a moment, then glanced at Sheba. Her face remained impassive. 'No, I don't think so, Ben,' he answered slowly. 'You get on home. I'll call your cell if I need you.'

'Very good, sir. Have a good night.' He turned and spoke quickly to Sheba, thanking her for the offer of a drink, but explaining that he wanted to get home to see his wife. This was his third late night in four days.

'Charlie keeps you busy, I see?' She laughed. 'Well, you sleep well tonight, Ben. I don't think he'll be disturbing you.' And the way the words just slipped from her lips and nestled themselves against Charlie's heart, he knew that he wouldn't. And then they entered the mansion and so much blood had flooded from his brain to his loins that he did not even register the art that dripped pricelessly from frames that cost more than he'd ever owned, the furniture that was already old while his own antiques were still saplings in a field. All he knew was that he wanted this woman and, though something told him now that she'd been spinning him a line all evening long – that she could probably buy him and his empire with the small change in her handbag – she wanted him.

One hand was down the front of his pants as she led him down a softly carpeted hallway; her mouth was on his as she opened a door and they tumbled backwards inside, groping in a darkness that was all the more profound for the stillness that clung to every surface, as though the entire room was furnished and painted in velvet, and Charlie felt himself trying to moderate his breathing so as not to even scratch the sublime beauty of that silence.

In darkness he heard her removing her dress; saw the occasional spark of static electricity as the fabric brushed against her dark-brown hair. Then it was his turn, pulling at his tie as she hauled at his waistband, and there was a sudden scratching sound as the fabric tore and a four-figure pair of suit trousers were condemned to oblivion. But she did not speak and he did not need to; he felt her hands on his flesh and her breath as well, and, though he reached out to touch her as she continued touching him, he was not even surprised as she slipped from his grasp. He'd have his turn, he heard her whisper, although how could she speak when her mouth was so full?

He closed his eyes despite the darkness, willing himself not to come. Every movement, every sensation, every flick of her tongue brought him closer and closer to the edge of ecstasy, and the more he fought against that final step, the more he knew it was a losing battle. He wondered whether he should warn her, but, when he raised his head and went to speak, the words would not come because it was already too late – too late to stop himself coming, and too late, too, for him to say anything else, for now she was twisting herself around alongside him, her hands on his forehead, her loins at his lips and her flavour, sweet spicy, already on his tongue.

171

She lay on her back, her legs parted wide; he was kneeling between them, his hands on her ass, raising her up so his neck didn't crick. He thought of asking if there was a pillow at hand, but balked at making so mundane a request; he would make love to her now and worry about the neck ache in the morning. But, almost as though she read his thoughts, her body shifted, raised and hung poised, her pussy warm and wet against his throat and he was about to bury his face in her folds when he heard a faint click, then felt pressure and pain. It felt as if she were biting him, and that old joke about women with teeth in their cunts flashed through his mind as he fought for another, more real explanation. But there was none, for there were teeth, and more than that, there were fangs. And, as they drained the blood from his veins, and the life from his body and his soul from existence, another thought planted itself in his brain, a single thought, a single word, that was the last thing his mind ever did before it blinked out.

* * *

He didn't understand it, but it was there all the same. That word was V-male.

A new breed of vampire was on the march.

And she worked in my library.